Book Six in the Nestled Hollow Romance series

Copyright © 2019, 2023 by Meg Easton

Cover Illustration by Covers and Cupcakes

Interior Design by Mountain Heights Publishing

Author website: www.megeaston.com

"Sweet romance at its best!
I want to visit Nestled Hollow over and over again!"

-ELANA JOHNSON
USA Today bestselling author of the *Hawthorn Harbor*
series and the *Getaway Bay* series

"Romance done right! Already looking forward to the next
Nestled Hollow love story. This series is going to be a
keeper!"

-KIMBERLY KREY
Best-selling author of the *Sweet Montana Brides* series

Love Started

It Started with a Sunset

It Started with a Note

It Started with a Glance

Coming Home to Silver Leaf Falls

more than enemies on the
bridge of main street

more than enemies on the bridge of main street

A NESTLED HOLLOW ROMANCE

MEG EASTON

contents

one

ZANE

The first thing that Zane Collins noticed when he took the Nestled Hollow exit off I-70 was the burn scar on the mountain right above the town. Man, that fire had gotten dangerously close to the homes. This was his second time seeing it— the first time had been when he'd come for an interview— but it still hit him just as hard now. This town definitely needed him to help them to be prepared for future disasters.

He drove his truck up First and then turned onto Main Street. The day was sunny and even though it was barely September, the weather was still a little on the cool side. Yet still, people were on the sidewalks, shopping and stopping to talk to neighbors as they passed, like they lived in some TV movie and all knew each other. He shook his head and chuckled. They probably did all know each other— this town was pretty small.

"*Our* town," he said out loud and reached out to rub Ranger's neck—his yellow lab that sat next to him. "That is going to take some getting used to."

He wondered if he would ever feel like this was his town without having to correct himself. He was thrilled to be the new Fire Chief and Emergency Management Director, but he never would've chosen to be in a small town. He had liked living in Springvale, Missouri—it was a big enough city that if you met people on the street, you probably didn't know them, and they'd respect you enough to ignore you.

He ran into burning buildings for a living; he could handle living in a small town. This was just a step on the ladder to becoming the Emergency Management Director of a bigger city, then of a state capital. And like every step he'd already taken on this ladder, he was going to give this step— this town— everything he had.

He pulled into a parking space in front of the Nestled Hollow Fire Department at the far end of Main Street. He had met Chief Stockton, the fire chief he would be replacing, when he had interviewed with him; Mayor Stone, who, in a quirk of small-town leadership, also doubled as the city manager; and the three members of the city council.

He was pretty sure that one of the city council

members doubled as a principal at one of the schools, one was over city recreation, and one owned the gas station. He should've expected as much when he saw that the position was for both the Fire Chief and the Emergency Management Director.

"Heel, Ranger," he said when he got out of the truck, and Ranger, like the good boy he was, hopped out onto the sidewalk and stuck at his side. Zane clipped the leash to his collar, even though if there was any dog who didn't need a leash, it was Ranger.

As soon as he walked through the door of the fire station, Chief Stockton met him and shook his hand. "Nice to see you again, Zane." The guy had a solid handshake but wasn't bone-crushing like he was overcompensating or taking out his aggressions on Zane's hand.

Chief Stockton was probably in his early sixties, but still seemed fairly fit. He knew that it wasn't entirely the Chief's choice that he was taking an early retirement, but the guy didn't seem to hold it against Zane that he was the one taking over his position. "Let me introduce you to everyone."

Chief Stockton led him around the ridiculously small station. Zane had been assigned to the main fire station in Springvale, but he had also spent some time in the other eleven stations in different fire districts throughout the city. None of them were as small as this place was.

He had to remind himself that this wasn't a step down in his career. Having the title of Fire Chief and Emergency Management Director was important to his plans, and this town desperately needed his skills.

He made it a point to remember the names of the firefighters and EMTs as Chief Stockton introduced him to each person. He was going to be their boss starting tomorrow, and he wasn't about to look incompetent in front of them.

There were seven men and women in all, and part of him guessed that this was the entirety of his crew and that they probably weren't all full-time employees, either. This was going to be interesting. Especially because the looks they were giving him were friendly on the outside, but anything but just beneath the surface. They were not happy to see their chief leaving.

That was okay. He didn't need them to love him; he needed them to help him get this town prepared. That was all that mattered.

"What do you say we start by checking out the damage on the mountain?" Chief Stockton asked, and led him and Ranger to a side-by-side with the NHFD logo on the side. Then they took it right out on the streets like it was a registered road vehicle and drove it toward the mountains. Apparently, that was another perk of living in a small town.

As they drove, Zane asked the chief about each

member of the fire department. He had spent countless hours preparing a plan for Nestled Hollow, but he hadn't known enough about the people who would be under him to know what kind of strengths he had to work with.

The closer they got to the mountain, the more he could see exactly where the fire line was. A walking path ran along the edge of the mountain, separating it from the houses, and in some areas, the path had been all that stopped the fire. In the worst spot, the fire had burned to within twenty feet of a couple of homes. It was alarming enough that Ranger even gave a soft whimper at seeing it.

"Do you know how the fire started?"

Chief Stockton nodded as he turned the vehicle onto the dirt walking path. "Some folks who were here for a weekend camping trip didn't put their campfire out completely. With as wet as spring was, the grasses had grown plenty, and when they dried out in that heat wave we had last month, it became the perfect kindling."

Zane held in his frustration at the carelessness of some people. "How many acres burned?"

The Chief turned onto a trail leading upward. "We got word of the fire quickly, and my team worked hard. Mountain Springs and Silver Stone each sent a couple of trucks and half a dozen firefighters before we got help from the county, so we got a handle on it pretty quickly. It still got one hundred and seven acres, though. So, big, but not massive."

Chief Stockton pulled the side-by-side to a stop, and Zane got out to inspect things a little more. He wished he would've been there to help fight the fire. The mountain was relatively steep, and although several big pines had been burned too badly to stay alive, they still stood.

But the bigger problem was that the underbrush was completely gone. "This winter is supposed to have heavy snowfall," Zane said. "Get a couple of warm days in the spring, especially if it combines with a spring rain, and there's a guaranteed landslide."

The Chief nodded. Of course, he knew all this— it was probably why he was willing to let the county officials push him into taking an early retirement.

Zane's mind was constantly filled with all the things that needed to happen in order to keep a city safe and protected in case of a natural disaster. It had been that way since he had worked his way to become a firefighter on assignment as assistant to the Emergency Management Director in Springvale a year and a half ago. Doing everything he had for Springvale had thrilled him. Made him feel alive.

After he looked at the damage on the mountain, he turned to see the town of Nestled Hollow laid out below it and ideas filled his mind at breakneck speed. There was so much he could do here. Energy coursed through him.

He wasn't taking over as Fire Chief officially until tomorrow, but he wanted to get things started today. This town was open and vulnerable, and there was so much to do to get it safe and protected.

"Do you have an apartment yet?"

The chief's question was so far from what he had been thinking, that it jolted him back to the present. "Um, no. Not until this weekend. I'm staying at All Nestled Inn for a few days."

"Leaving behind family in Springvale?"

"A brother." Technically, his brother lived in Georgia, not far from their childhood home where their parents still lived. Their parents hadn't been around much in Zane's childhood and were around even less in his adulthood, so it was easier to just mention Wyatt.

"Are you close?"

"No. We just reconnected a year ago."

"Gonna miss your old city?"

He glanced at the Fire Chief to see why he was being interrogated, then looked back at the city. The look on the man's face showed he was just being friendly. "I really enjoyed getting that place ready for any disaster. But I'm ready to move on to another city where I can help."

"No girlfriend?"

A chuckle escaped him. "Nope." His last girlfriend had broken up with him six months ago because he was "emotionally unavailable." He hadn't been looking since.

"You ready to take on this job?"

"Very." He was itching to start getting an emergency

system in place. If he could talk the Chief into handing over the job today, he would take over this minute.

Chief Stockton stood next to him, and both men looked out over the city, arms crossed, legs in a wide stance. After a long silence, the Chief said, "Look out for this city." His voice was filled with enough emotion that Zane's eyes flew to the man for a second. "You're an outsider, so you might have an uphill climb. But they're good people. Take care of them."

Zane knew that he was by far the best man for the job, and he took his job seriously. So with complete confidence, he turned to the Chief and said, "I will." Then shook his hand, sealing the promise.

———

Zane dropped Ranger off at an animal boarding shop named Paws and Relax just two buildings down from the fire station and gave him a good neck rub. "I'll be back to get you in the morning. I just need you to stay here for three nights, and then you'll get to come home with me. You can handle three nights, right?"

Ranger gave his bark that always sounded like an enthusiastic "Yep!"

"You're a good boy, Ranger." He nodded at the woman who was working at the shop, and she immediately crouched down to talk to his dog and give him a good pet. He'd be okay here.

Then he moved his truck from one of the few parking spots in front of the fire station to the parking lot behind All Nestled Inn, even though the two buildings were just over a block apart.

As he carried in his luggage, he wished this town had a Marriott, a Hilton, or even a Best Western. A place where the person at the front desk would exchange pleasantries with him when he walked in and then would forget about him for the rest of his stay. At a place like All Nestled Inn, they'd probably want to get in his business and be chatty, and he had work to do.

As soon as he walked into the hotel lobby, his eyes were drawn to one thing— the woman on top of a tall ladder, changing a lightbulb in the middle of the tall-ceilinged room while talking on the phone.

And she stood one step higher on the ladder than was safe —on the step that he knew said, "No climbing or standing."

In a skirt.

What was she thinking, being that high up on a ladder in a skirt? At least she had left her heels on the floor at the bottom of the ladder. She was talking on the phone to an HVAC repairman, from what he could tell, holding the phone with her shoulder, while holding a lightbulb in one hand, unscrewing the old one from the fixture with the other, leaning against the ladder for what little support the top shelf of it could provide.

He wanted to ask if she needed help, but she hadn't seen him yet, and he was worried that saying something might just surprise her enough to make her fall off the ladder. So he just watched in silence. And, okay, maybe checked her out a little.

She was dressed in a fancy pink blouse and had long, straight dark hair that fell to the middle of her back. And that skirt that hugged a very nice figure. After removing the old lightbulb, she shifted on the ladder while she switched each lightbulb to the opposite hand, and then began screwing in the new one.

"Tony," she said, her voice firm. "You know that there are nights this time of year when it starts to get a little chilly. Especially because most visitors aren't used to Nestled Hollow's cooler temperatures."

She paused a moment, then said in a nicer voice, one that was part teasing and part sweet-talking, "You can find a time to come fix it in this one room, can't you?"

Part of him wanted to give her a lecture about safety. The other part of him— the part that was winning, surprisingly— just admired her efficiency and her willingness to be up on the ladder when she obviously hadn't planned on doing it today, based on her choice of outfit.

Another pause, then she said, "That's why you're the

best, Tony. See you tomorrow." She finished screwing in the bulb, then grabbed the phone with her free hand, pressed the button to end the call, then, with the burnt-out lightbulb in one hand and phone in the other, started climbing down the ladder.

And that's when she noticed him and let out a shout of surprise and flinched enough that the ladder shook and she grabbed hold tightly, dropping the lightbulb and the cell phone she had been holding. Zane had been on alert for danger from the moment he had walked into the lobby, so he stepped forward and caught the lightbulb before it crashed to the floor.

"You scared me!"

"I tried not to."

The woman made her way down the last few steps of the ladder. Then she slipped her heels on and smoothed down the front of her skirt. "Well," she said, chuckling, "at least now we know how I'd react if someone broke into my house." Her voice was nice. Pleasant, but with something else, too. Mischievousness, maybe.

"It's a good tactic— scream and drop whatever you're holding. You might be able to scare off an attacker with that." He handed her the lightbulb. "But I didn't break in. I wasn't even trying to be quiet."

"I could see the hallways to the guest rooms and the parking lot from the ladder, so I thought I'd know if someone came in." She looked him up and down. "You're a big, strong guy. I wouldn't have expected you to come in so ninja-quiet."

He smiled. So she was noticing him, too. "And I didn't expect to find a woman mid-lightbulb emergency when I came to check in."

She bent down and picked up her cell phone with her free hand, turning it over to check for damage, and then met his eyes again. "Well, one can never predict when one might have a lightbulb emergency. That's why it's good to be prepared."

She was speaking his language. Even if there were so many things wrong with what she had considered "prepared."

"And the phone call? Did that come mid-emergency?"

"Nah. I was just trying to kill two birds with one stone." Then she headed to the check-in desk. "Or, well, I guess three birds. Am I checking you out?" She paused mid-step as she rounded the desk, and then turned toward him, cheeks flushed a bright pink. "I'm sorry. Am I checking you *in*. To the hotel. I mean, obviously— you've got your luggage and everyone checking out has already checked out."

Her face was getting redder and redder the more she talked. He chuckled and kind of wished she would just keep going.

She shook her head and set down the phone and the lightbulb. "Maybe we should just start over. Hi, my name is Alete Keetch." She held out her hand and he shook it. Hers was also a very nice handshake— as strong as Chief Stockton's, but so much softer than his calloused hands. "Welcome to All Nestled Inn. Will you be staying with us long?"

He couldn't help the smile that kept tugging at him. "Three days."

"Well then, let's get you checked *in* so you can get to your room."

Maybe, just maybe, he thought as he watched Alete work, *living in Nestled Hollow wouldn't be so bad.*

two

ALETE

"He did not," Alete said to her front desk attendant, Judy, as they chatted about Judy's date the night before. She picked up another towel from the laundry bin and folded it.

"True story," Judy said. "And then he said, 'Did the sun come out, or did you just smile at me?'"

"And," Alete prompted, not knowing whether to give a positive or a negative response. She could never tell if Judy's stories would have a happy or a sad ending until she finished.

"And then I decided I didn't want to have that awkward end-of-date 'should we kiss or should we not' moment. So I grabbed hold of his shoulders, pulled him toward me, and planted a kiss smack on his lips."

Alete laughed, and Judy looked around like she'd been

so engrossed in her story that she hadn't remembered that they had the door of one of the back rooms open so they could see the lobby as they folded the hotel towels. "Why, again, are we folding the towels? Is Morgan not coming in?"

"No, she is," Alete said. "I just figured we'd give her a head start."

Judy put a hand on her hip and gave Alete a flat look. She was just opening her mouth, probably to give Alete a stern talking to, when a guest walked into the lobby, looking like she needed something. Alete set the towel down that she had been folding and took one step toward the couple when Judy used the hand that had been on her hip to stop Alete. "Helping them is *my* job. Quit being a thief."

Judy headed toward the front of the inn, stepping around George as he walked in her direction carrying a ladder. "Hey, boss. Where's that burnt-out light?"

"Oh, don't worry about it. I took care of it last night."

"Boss," George said, his voice a pained pleading. "I told you I would only be gone one day. You didn't have to go and take all my work."

Judy came walking back down the hall just in time to hear his comment. "Trisha and Pete didn't show up for tennis this morning, did they?"

Alete rolled her eyes, knowing exactly where this conversation was going. "It's Thursday."

"Right. So, I guess that means—" Judy glanced up at the ceiling, thinking, before meeting Alete's eyes again, "—Roger and those guys didn't show up for flag football."

"It got canceled. But," she added, before Judy could blame all of her extra energy on that, "I did go for a run instead."

Judy looked at George, and George snapped his fingers. "It's September. She's always this way in September."

"Don't you have a soccer practice to coach?" Judy's hands fluttered, grasping for an invisible something in the air. "Or accounting to do?"

All Nestled Inn did enough business that she could very much justify having the employees she had. She was glad that she could provide jobs for people in the community. And she knew it was important for them to be able to actually do their jobs. She never meant to take over— it just happened.

Alete set down the towel she had been about to fold. "No, but I do need to run and see my parents before the Main Street Business Alliance meeting this afternoon. Will you guys hold down the fort?"

She headed out of the building and to the pedestrian bridge that went over Snowdrift Springs, the stream that ran right down the middle of Main Street, and then walked two buildings up to Keetch's Burgers and Shakes, her family's business. She skipped right past the hostess podium and seated herself at the bar where her mom was making shakes.

"Hey, sweetie. Middle of the afternoon on a Thursday. I'm guessing you're here because you ran out of things to do?"

Alete threw her folded arms onto the bar. "I'm just so…itchy this time of year." She helped out with the Fall Market every year in October, and she was always the lead on the Thankful for You event, but there wasn't anything that could be done with either of those that she hadn't already done.

Helping her town was just what she did, so when there didn't seem to be anything to help with, everything felt wrong. "Why are there no town celebrations in September? Nothing happens this month. Why? Why would we have a month of nothing?"

"Maybe you should plan something."

"I should. Because I may have to start a chain of hotels or something if I don't get a bit of a challenge in my life soon." Which she'd actually never do. Her roots in Nestled Hollow ran so deep that she couldn't have a job that took her out of the town that much.

She glanced through the big front windows of the restaurant to where the fire had scarred the mountain a month before. She wished she could do something to fix that. The fire had burned fast and strong like it was attacking her city.

It had been scary at the time, and she'd helped out by housing as many people whose homes were threatened by the fire as she could in the inn, and she even let a family with a new baby move into her own apartment during the evacuations. She was so busy at the inn that she knew she'd be spending most of her time there anyway.

But now, looking at that mountain, it wasn't scary; it was sad. There were small signs of new growth, but not much yet. She knew that winter snows would be covering it in a few months, and then things would really start growing again in the spring, but for now, it was a reminder of how bad things got.

"What about planning a retirement party for Chief Stockton?"

Alete shook her head. "Already thought of that and checked. The fire department, police department, and city employees are planning it together and don't need any help."

Her mom shrugged. "You could slow down. Not be so efficient. Be like a normal person and get overwhelmed by running an entire hotel yourself and go home every night stressed out."

"Ha ha," she said as her dad came around the corner from the kitchen to join the conversation.

"I don't think she could slow down if she tried." He smiled at Alete as he put an arm around her mom. "We knew you were going to be a go-getter when you were three and wanted to do every sport that existed. And when you hit first grade and were old enough to play flag football and didn't care that you were the only girl on the team."

"Or," her mom added, "when you rolled the biggest watermelons out of the garden to the street and set up a stand selling watermelon slices. You were *six*."

Alete didn't remember it well, but she'd heard the story and had seen the pictures.

"I still remember the sign you made," her dad said, motioning with his hand like he was spreading it out in the air in front of them. "'Watermelon slices, twenty-five cents.' And then right below it, it said, 'slice your own, because I'm too young to use the knife.'" He paused the story, laughing, and then added, "And most of the words were spelled wrong because you were six and didn't want to ask how to spell them."

"Because then you'd have to tell me you were selling my watermelons," her mom said.

Alete shook her head. She had heard the story quite a few times, and now the eight or so people who were sitting at tables eating a late lunch had heard it, too.

"Yep," her dad said. "Even back then you needed plenty of things to keep you busy."

"You could start dating someone," both of her parents said at the same time. *Both*. The exact same wording. The exact same time. And then they both laughed at saying the same thing *again*. It was like their brains were so in sync that they probably didn't even have to say things out loud when it was just the two of them.

"Dating," Alete said, giving them a flat look. "*That's* your solution?"

"Now don't give us that look, honey," her mom said. "We've already got two daughters-in-law, a son-in-law, and three grandkids from your siblings and will probably get a lot more. We've accepted that you aren't going to be giving us another son-in-law or grandkids anytime soon, if at all. But you've dated lots of guys that you've had good times with. Maybe that's what you need."

"I said I wanted a challenge. A way to help people in Nestled Hollow. Not that I wanted to be annoyed or to learn more patience or have someone dictating my time for me."

Even though she felt like she had to give her parents grief for bringing up dating, her mind had immediately gone to Zane Collins, the man who she'd embarrassed herself in front of the night before. Now that was one good-looking man. Lean, but with toned muscles that even showed through his jacket. Adorable smile. A fire in his eyes. Quick to joke around. Even though she had only been with him for a few minutes, it was enough to make her intrigued.

Enough to hope several times since then that he would walk through the lobby on his way somewhere while she was there so they could chat more. Hopefully at a time when she wasn't dropping things and saying exactly the wrong phrase.

Too bad the guy said he was only staying there three days. One of the biggest drawbacks of her job was that the people she met were only in town for a few days. It wasn't the best job for meeting potential dates.

"Okay, okay," her mom said. "We won't push you. Are you coming to the Main Street Business Alliance meeting this afternoon? Mayor Stone was in here an hour ago—the meeting is going to be combined with the City Council meeting." Her voice seemed to have something else behind it like maybe this conversation wasn't as much about changing the subject away from dating as it seemed. "He says the new fire chief just got into town and he's going to present his emergency plan at the meeting."

And there it was. But it did make her sit up taller. That sounded interesting.

"I just wish Chief Stockton wasn't being pushed out of his position," Evia, the older woman who was sitting with her husband at a nearby table, said. "The chief is such a good guy."

Alete turned in her stool toward Evia. "What do you know about the new chief?"

Instead of Evia answering, Don Williards did, from another table. "I heard that he's half as old as you'd expect and twice as intense."

Half as old as you'd expect. This combined meeting was sounding more and more interesting.

Misty, who was lunching with her church ladies' group, was already turned in their direction. "Intense, indeed. My grandson's on the fire department, you know, and he says that the whole department has been on their toes ever since the guy came in for his interview."

"Anyone know his name?" Alete asked.

Everyone shook their head except Misty. She reached into her purse and pulled out her phone. "Let's see. My Jarred texted it earlier." She looked down, silent for a few moments, while everyone— even the people who hadn't joined in the conversation—turned in her direction, waiting for her answer. A smile of triumph at having found it lit her face a moment before she said, "Zane Collins."

Alete turned back around in her seat, a smile spreading across her face. Things were definitely getting interesting.

three

ZANE

Zane woke up sweating, shaking, breathing heavily, and nearly certain he had been screaming moments ago. He glanced at the clock on the hotel night stand— the red numbers showed it was just past two. Hopefully, he didn't wake up everyone in the hotel.

Knowing he couldn't just fall back asleep after a dream like that, especially with his heart racing so fast, he got out of bed and walked over to his small second-floor window, trying to shake off the dream. The nightmares didn't come so often now. He had been a thirteen-year-old kid when the break-in happened, and he was a twenty-nine-year-old man now— he shouldn't still be having nightmares inspired by it.

Not that it was only about the break-in. In this one, he had been a kid, walking hand-in-hand with someone he trusted. Now that he was awake, he couldn't remember who, but in the dream, he had felt safe, protected. Somewhere that felt like home.

Then, without warning, a tornado hit the house. But unlike the time when he was nine and home alone when one neared his house, this time he was with someone he trusted. The tornado swirled and twisted and roared violently around him, and he watched as everything important to him was sucked into its funnel.

And then he had started rising off the ground, being lifted by the wind. The person he had trusted was still on the ground but had let go of his hand. He wasn't pulled out of their grasp— they had simply let go. He didn't swirl around in the tornado as all his things did, but he was still trapped there, flailing his arms and legs a good ten feet above the ground. The motions did nothing to help him get back down. He was powerless.

That's when he'd woken up. The dream hadn't been about a break-in at all, but he was left with the same feeling of a trust broken, important things missing, control taken away. He ran his fingers through his hair and forced himself to take slow, deep breaths and think calming thoughts. He had a big day tomorrow, and he needed sleep.

———

"What's your goal at this meeting?" the Ex-chief Stockton asked Zane as they sat in the office that, as of nine a.m. this morning when he was sworn in, was now Zane's.

Zane put all his notes into the folder. "To get the city council and Main Street Business Alliance to help get the town on board with my plans." That really was the entirety of his goal. He wasn't required to meet with them and go over his plan, but this town could be in some serious danger and things would go much more smoothly if they all cooperated.

Stockton sat on a mini fridge in the corner of the much too small office, his arms folded, and nodded at the papers Zane was gathering. "You gonna present all of that today?"

"Planning to."

The old chief just nodded, and he could tell that the man didn't agree. Stockton had consented to come in for a few hours each day for the next two weeks to show Zane the ropes and answer any questions before he officially retired. It was helpful in some situations. Less so when Stockton looked at him like he couldn't pull something off.

"What," he said, his annoyance making the question come out as a demand.

Stockton shrugged, still keeping his arms crossed, which Zane realized was the default for the guy. "It's just," he paused, "a lot."

"Yeah, it is. They need a lot."

"*They?*"

Zane closed his eyes and breathed in slowly. "We," he said. He had to remember to say *we* during the meeting.

From the updates he'd gotten from Stockton and Mayor Stone, he realized that he was basically starting at Step One with this town. They didn't have any official emergency plans beyond things that the fire department and police department did on a situation-by-situation basis. Nothing for big disasters and their town could potentially have a lot of those. They desperately needed protection. They were like a baby kitten left all alone with a pack of wolves circling, and he felt his muscles tightening and a burning drive to help them.

He had gone through the town budget, county and state emergency preparedness information, and all the resources about Nestled Hollow he could get his hands on before he arrived in town and during the past twenty-four hours. He'd come up with a decent plan to accomplish the huge task of preparing them against the myriad of dangers potentially facing them. One he was proud of. With what he had to work with, it was pretty impressive, and he was very ready to put it into place. Anything he could do to speed up the process of getting them strong and secure and protected he was going to do.

Once he had everything together, he said, "Come on, boy," and he bent down and rubbed the sides of Ranger's neck before he attached the leash. Then he, Stockton, and Ranger walked from the fire station at the end of Main Street to the library, which was right next door to the hotel he was staying in. Zane hadn't been to the library yet, so Stockton led the way around to the back of the building and down the two steps to the back door.

They were about ten minutes early, but already the room was filled with a lot of people, all standing in groups, chatting. As they walked into the room, all eyes fell on Zane, then went to Ranger, then Stockton, and then back to Zane, and he felt the weight of their appraisal of him.

Zane put on a smile and nodded a greeting to the two groups they passed as Stockton led him to the row of seven chairs at the front of the room that faced all the rest of the chairs. Six of the people he guessed would be sitting in those seats were standing in a circle, chatting. Mayor Stone, the three city council members whose faces he recognized but whose names he had forgotten since his initial interview, and two people he hadn't met. He assumed the seventh chair was for him.

"Hello, everyone," Stockton said. "I would like to introduce you to the new Fire Chief and Emergency Management Director, Zane Collins, and his fire dog, Ranger." Stockton motioned to the mayor. "You've met Mayor Stone, of course."

Zane nodded and shook the man's hand.

"And you remember city council members Principal Ploeger, Shavonna, and Riley."

He shook each of their hands in turn, grateful that Stockton mentioned their names again, helping him to avoid an awkward situation. For as much as the man had the ability to make his life miserable here, especially after getting forced out of his position, he didn't. He'd earned Zane's respect.

"And this is Ed and Linda Keetch. They run the Main Street Business Alliance."

Keetch. That had been the last name of the intriguing woman on the ladder that he'd met the night before and frequently thought of today. As he shook their hands, he said, "Any relation to Alete?"

Surprise showed on their faces before Linda said, "She's our daughter. She didn't tell us that the two of you had met."

Her eyes darted across the room, so Zane turned, too, and saw Alete chatting with a group of people. Of course, she would be there— she ran a business that was on Main Street. He should've realized.

She must have felt his gaze on her because she looked in his direction and gave him a smile that made him want to ignore everyone else and go chat with her. Thoughts of her had interrupted his work enough times since their meeting last night that he wanted to get to know her more.

He smiled back. They hadn't chatted for long, but he was glad she would see him in action today. If there was one thing he was confident about, it was his expertise in preparing a town against disasters.

He forced his eyes to leave Alete and go back to her mother. He should've guessed these were her parents. Alete had her mom's strong cheekbones and her dad's spirited, bright eyes. "Alete and I met last night when I checked in at All Nestled Inn."

As he made small talk with the Keetchs and the town leaders, he tried to assess each of their strengths and weaknesses. He was going to need to assign a lot of tasks, and he wanted to make sure he chose the right people for the jobs. And, he had to admit, he might have spent a little time trying to assess Alete through what he was learning about her parents.

A couple of minutes before four o'clock, they all took their seats at the front of the room, Ranger dutifully sitting at attention next to him at the end of the row of chairs. All the chatting groups broke up and found their seats, too.

He looked out across the room for any signs of danger, like he always did, and found his eyes landing on Alete. She sat in the front row next to a woman in a blazer over a t-shirt that said, "Oh, crop" with a symbol he didn't recognize. Alete was wearing slacks today, and she looked just as amazing in them as she had in the skirt. Her hair was pulled up, but somehow, even with her nice clothes, it didn't look like it was up to be fancy. It looked like it was up because she had work to do and wanted to get down to business. He liked it.

Both Ed and Linda Keetch got up to start the meeting and talked about Main Street Business Alliance things. As the older couple talked back and forth with the group, he studied the crowd. They all seemed to be pretty easy going and went for anything the couple said. Good.

And then he found his eyes back on Alete. Hers seemed to find his just as often, and she smiled at him like they shared a secret. Normally, he didn't seek out the most intriguing, beautiful woman in the room. Normally, he stayed focused on whatever job he was there to do and only focused on people to the extent that he needed them to do a job.

But normally, Alete wasn't in the room. Something about this woman seemed to draw him in. He glanced down at the folder in his hands just to get his head back in the game.

The Keetchs talked about some fall market thing they had coming up next month. It sounded like one of the many unnecessary celebrations he had seen on the list of town events, but the more the older couple talked, the more he realized that this was one of the ones meant to bring in tourists, which he knew was important to their economy. And besides, it didn't take from the town budget at all— the costs seemed to be covered by the Business Alliance.

His leg started bouncing up and down and Ranger noticed, so he stilled his leg. He had only been in his new position for seven hours. But this town was currently exposed to possible threats, and he needed to be doing something about it. It had been nearly twenty minutes since the meeting began, and he hadn't needed to be here for any of this. He could've been getting some of the piles of work done that were waiting for him in his office.

Finally, the Keetchs sat down and Mayor Stone got up and introduced him to the group as the new Fire Chief and the Emergency Management Director. "So I guess you can call him Chief Collins, or Director Collins, or 'Hey you in the NHFD shirt.'" The mayor chuckled at his own comment. "Anyway, let's give him a warm welcome."

Everyone clapped as Zane stood and walked to the middle of the open area at the front and placed his folder on the small table off to the side. Ranger came and sat next to him, showing what a good, obedient boy he was. When Ranger had been retired from the Springvale Fire Department and became his dog full-time, he knew the dog had missed the action. He was glad Ranger could be back on duty again.

Zane told me about where he was from and what he had done in Springvale that had qualified him for this job. He wanted them to know that he was an expert in his field. He didn't miss that Alete had raised an eyebrow, impressed.

Then he talked about the fire on the mountain, and how it was almost an inevitability that there was going to be a landslide in the spring and that they had many other natural disasters that were a very real possibility because of where they lived.

"Now, there are lots of things I'll be doing with county and state officials to help us prepare, but what I want to talk to you all about is what I need your help to do. Right now, Nestled Hollow has no emergency plan. Zilch. That's just asking for trouble. Your town is vulnerable and completely unprepared, and you're lucky that things didn't go seriously wrong with that fire."

He noticed Alete stiffen, along with several other people. A couple of them crossed their arms. He didn't care if his words made them defensive. They needed to understand the gravity of their situation.

"You've got an awful evacuation plan, no plan for displaced families, virtually no official communications in place, and almost no emergency equipment."

"Now to be fair," a middle-aged man with a bit of a paunch said, "we did take care of everyone who needed to evacuate. Alete at All Nestled Inn and Carl at Home Suite Home took in people. Anyone they couldn't fit, others took in. We looked out for each other."

"All I can say is, you got lucky. With no emergency

plans in place, you could've just as easily had mass casualties. I'm going to change that."

He realized that he'd just thrown Stockton under the bus. He couldn't worry about that right now, though. He'd only been in this town for a day, but he didn't want to see it overcome by a major natural disaster. When the next thing hit— and it would, even if it wasn't soon—he wanted them to be as safe and as prepared as possible.

"There's a lot we need to do. Everything from having families decide where to meet in an emergency, to running practice drills, to getting people CERT trained. Your Search and Rescue gear is decent, and with as close as you are to the mountains, it sounds like the fire department has had to use it a fair number of times, especially with all the tourists you get."

A few people chuckled at that. He was beginning to realize that one of the main duties of the Nestled Hollow Fire Department wasn't so much putting out fires, but finding people who had gotten themselves lost or stuck or found themselves unprepared in the mountains. Honestly, he had no idea how they could even be successful working with only what they had here.

"It's not enough, though. You—" he paused and corrected himself, "—*we* need incident command trailers and mobile command stations and radio communications if we want to pull this town's preparedness into this century."

Every time his eyes fell on Alete, he saw a fiery passion burning in her eyes. But it didn't look like worry over the realization that they were so vulnerable or excitement at the prospect of getting her town safe and protected. Her expression almost looked angry, but he didn't understand why. She should be afraid for her town because they were potentially in a lot of danger. Was he not getting that across? Surely she wanted to keep everyone safe. She should be jumping to her feet, asking what she could do to help.

A guy in his early thirties who looked pretty decently fit called out, "All that costs money. Where's it going to come from?"

He had planned to spell out all the steps the town needed to go through to get prepared and talk about all the things they needed so they'd be one hundred percent on board and ready to pay for anything before he got to the how. But he had also come to this meeting prepared to alter the order as it seemed appropriate. They could skip to costs.

He opened his folder and took out the paper where he'd worked everything out. It had been tough to come up with the money when he was working with such a small town budget, but it was a solid plan that he stood behind.

"Grants and donations will cover part of it, hopefully. But since most of these items haven't been purchased over time, as you'd hope, there's a lot that's needed. Grants and donations won't cover everything.

"I've looked at the town budget, though, and we can come up with the difference by cutting frivolous things that don't matter when it comes to the big picture. Like some rec sports and town events that cost the town money— things like the Thankful for You event, the Fire and Ice Festival, the Take Flight Festival, and another event or two."

In a flash, Alete was out of her chair on the front row and standing right in front of him, fists clenched at her side, that fire burning in her eyes, looking like a mama bear about to pounce on something she thought was threatening her cubs. Ranger reacted almost as immediately, giving a warning bark and standing ready to attack if needed.

"It's okay, boy," he said, petting the dog's head to let him know Alete wasn't a threat, even though the furious look on her face told him that she very much was.

four

ALETE

Alete couldn't control her heart rate or the heat rushing through her body as she faced down Zane. "Are you being serious right now?"

She'd managed to do both through most of the meeting, which she should get some kind of award for. Especially when he kept saying how awful her town was at everything. Maybe they were on paper— she didn't know. But whether they had a paper spelling out a plan or not, they'd all reacted like pros when that fire had started. It hadn't all worked out simply because they were *lucky*. It all worked out because they came together to pull off something amazing.

They were a small town. Springvale was probably forty times their size. With resources like they must've had, of course, they could get all the supplies and equipment he mentioned. He shouldn't expect Nestled Hollow to have all that, and he shouldn't be acting like they were so inferior because they didn't.

But to suggest that their town celebrations were "frivolous" and didn't matter made her blood boil. She couldn't have stayed sitting in her seat if she had wanted to.

His body was turned halfway between her and the Main Street Business Alliance members, but his face was turned fully to her. A look of baffled shock crossed his expression for a small moment before his eyes narrowed, his stance rigid. "Of course I'm serious. The business of saving a town is very serious."

Alete narrowed her eyes, too. "There's more to keeping a town thriving than buying fancy equipment." There was so much more. It was the entire reason why she dedicated the bulk of her free time to helping her town with all the "frivolous" things. She was sure her expression showed the same baffled shock that he didn't get it.

And here she'd been making flirty eyes at him at the beginning of the meeting, imagining the possibility of the two of them dating now that she knew he was moving into a more permanent residence once he left All Nestled Inn. She couldn't believe that she'd been thinking of him all day and that she'd had dreams about him last night— dreams that she wasn't about to share with anyone.

He turned fully to her now, his legs planted in a wide

stance, but he stayed maddeningly calm, even though she could see the passion burning in his eyes. One hand was still on his dog, and the other hand was relaxed at his side, not clenched tightly in a fist like hers were.

"Answer me this, honestly," he said. "What do you think is more important: a town party, or people's lives?" His voice wasn't exactly calm and at a normal volume, but it wasn't shouting or angry, either. Which made her more upset, like he was trying to show that he, and by extension his words, were the better ones. Which they weren't, because he wasn't seeing the big picture.

She found herself clenching her jaw as she formulated her answer. "Those town parties are what bring people together and help them to look out for one another. We might not have had all your communications methods in place or the fancy equipment Springvale has, but when those fires hit, we looked out for each other, precisely *because of* town events."

"I'm sorry," he said, "but town parties just don't rank higher than safety."

Joey shouted out, "Just like in Maslow's Hierarchy!"

She didn't even spare Joey a glare; she just kept her eyes on Zane. Joey was the kind of guy who would've brought popcorn if he thought they would be getting a show like this. He was just trying to throw gasoline on the fire.

Zane didn't take his blazing eyes off her as he raised an

eyebrow and said, "The guy has a point. In Maslow's Hierarchy, safety and security come before love and belonging."

She narrowed her eyes at him as she shook her head. "They aren't steps. They intertwine more than you think. They fuel each other."

His nostrils flared and a vein in his neck pulsed, and somehow, the man still looked like he could be on the cover of a fireman calendar. From the corner of her eye, she could see that he was flexing his hand— almost coming to a fist, then stretching out, then repeating.

"First, people need to be safe. We need to teach everyone what to do in a disaster. They can't just expect someone will come along and help them out. They need to look out for themselves because they can't count on anyone else." He flinched when he said the last part, which told her he was speaking from personal experience and not just from a belief that each individual needed their own preparation.

"That is a sad way to live. The people here *can* count on others. That's why building a community is so important."

He stepped closer to her, his eyes burning into hers. "When people work hard to give others a physically safe space, it shows they love and care about them. When they don't—" He stopped mid-sentence, and just gave a shrug, insinuating that she must not care.

She stepped even closer to him, showing that she was not going to back down—she was going to match every step that he made. Her heart was pounding, sending super-heated blood throughout her body. He was probably a good eight inches taller than her. Thank heavens she was wearing high heels today so she could look him more directly in the eye. She hoped he saw a fierce, unyielding determination in hers. "When people work hard to give others an emotionally safe space, *that's* what shows they love and care about them."

The two of them stared each other down, less than a foot apart, hands on hips. Her pulse was so fast and strong that she could feel her own heartbeat. And she could feel a heat from him—a passion for what he was saying, coming off hot and strong.

But what he was saying was wrong.

"And I would say that you must not care about this town if you're not willing to sacrifice things to help them."

She didn't care about her town? Her breathing quickened and the heat that filled her body felt ready to burst free. Maybe he needed to see a record of how much time she spent helping this town. Not that one existed, but if it did, he would see that she put in more hours than anyone. Her parents and the mayor included.

"Kiss or get off the stage!" Joey called out. She did send a glare in his direction for that comment. This was not about that *at all*. This was one-hundred-percent about the man in front of her thinking he could waltz into their town, insult everyone, and then act like he knew everything about them and what they needed.

"Okay, okay," Mayor Stone said, pushing his way in between the two of them.

Alete broke eye contact with Zane and stepped a few feet away, hoping that her anger would subside, but knowing that she cared way too much about this town to let it. She looked out over the group of her fellow business owners and could see that they were just as worried about the direction Zane had been trying to lead them, too.

"This meeting has obviously come to a standstill," the mayor said. "I think it might be best to call it a day, give everyone some space, and then revisit this later."

"This town is in danger *now*," Zane growled. "We can't put off getting prepared."

Principal Ploeger stood up, his hands raised like he was approaching an injured animal. "Okay, how about this. Chief Collins, earlier in the meeting, you mentioned that one of the first things we should do is to have each family plan where they would meet in a disaster, right?"

Although Zane's angry glare had been fixed on her, he pulled his eyes away to look at the principal and nodded. "Each family needs to pick four meeting places. A safe place in their home if the danger is outside, a safe place outside of their home but in their neighborhood, somewhere in town if they can't get to their neighborhood, and an out-of-town meeting spot. And it's important to do drills so it's all second nature." His voice had started off angry and fast but was calmer by the end. Alete couldn't guarantee that her voice wouldn't still come out angry right now.

"All right," Principal Ploeger said. "How about I start something with my students at the elementary school? I'll send home a paper to have them figure out their family meeting spots and practice with them. If we get, say, ninety-five percent of kids who return it, signed that they've done it, I'll wear pajamas to school for a week or shave my head or something. How does that sound?"

Zane nodded and took a step back. He seemed to have gotten that he'd lost and should accept the consolation prize.

Good.

———

Alete stopped by the bakery and got four cinnamon rolls on her way to her parents' house. She always stopped by to see her grandma after the Main Street Business Alliance Meeting, and since she couldn't seem to shake the sour feeling she was left with after the meeting no matter how much she tried, she figured she should get something sweet to counter it.

"Ammie?" she called out as she opened the front door.

"Kitchen, Sunshine."

Alete walked into the kitchen where her grandma was washing some vegetables at the sink in the center island, the vegetables shaking slightly in her hands. "I brought us a treat," Alete said as she set down the container.

Her grandma looked between the veggies she was holding and the cinnamon rolls. Then she set the makings of dinner aside and said, "Life's short. We better eat the cinnamon rolls first."

Alete laughed and got plates out of the cupboard and forks out of the drawer, feeling her grandma's eyes on her the whole time. Knowing Ammie, she was probably trying to figure out what was bothering Alete.

"So," her grandma said, dragging out the word, yet trying to sound like it wasn't a loaded question, "have you met the new Fire Chief yet?"

"Yes," Alete said, the word coming out more like a growl.

"Hoohoohoo! I found out what slow car was in your fast lane in *one guess*." She licked a finger and placed a mark in the air. "Put one more in the win column for me."

Alete laughed. "He would've driven you nuts, too." She lifted a cinnamon roll onto each plate. "Not only did he insult our town, but he suggested we get rid of the Thankful for You event to pay for his plan."

Ammie gasped. "He didn't. Did you kick him in the shins?"

"Ammie."

"What? It sounds like he needed to be kicked in the shins."

This was why she had been telling her grandma her woes since she was a toddler. Ammie never tried to wipe away Alete's emotions—she would pick up her metaphorical pitchfork and stand at Alete's side, asking Alete to point her in the direction of the enemy. "Nope. Instead, I had a yelling match with him in front of the entire Main Street Business Alliance and City Council."

"*Then* did you kick him in the shins? You should've just brought your foot back real good and kicked him." She paused for a short moment, and then said, "Oh. He's good-lookin', huh? The kind of good lookin' that makes you daydream about him whenever the screen's taking too long to load or you're waiting in line at the grocery store?"

Alete nodded. "More so before he opened his mouth and started talking bad about our town. That dark hair with just the perfect amount of wave, that strong jaw, and those long lean muscles of his were so much more attractive before the meeting."

She carried the plates to the table. She heard an *oof!* from her grandma and turned around to see that she had struggled to get from the sink to the table and had caught herself with the kitchen counter.

"Ammie! If you don't want to wait for me to walk with

you, use your walker." Alete was at her grandma's side in an instant, her arm out in case she needed it for support.

"I hate that thing." She shuffled to the table, her right leg stiffer, as usual, and her right arm shaking slightly, but she got there without needing to rely on Alete's arm. The inner ear balance problem had come on fairly quickly in the past several weeks. The changes in her grandma's gait, though, were small and gradual, but she could tell that it was getting worse.

"I know, Ammie. But it's what will keep you from falling into something."

She flicked her hand like she was trying to shove away the comment. "Being incapable is worse than mosquitos at an outdoor wedding. I stayed active my entire life precisely to avoid this."

"Well, hopefully, your new medication will kick in soon and you'll be good as new. Maybe we can even get you that fancy brain thing. And then you'll really kick Parkinson's disease in the shins."

Ammie laughed. "Can we kick it in the shins a lot of times, just to get the point across? With shoes on? I don't want to give it the satisfaction of making me stub my toe. Then, if I'm still in the mood, you can take me to meet the hot Fire Chief, and I can kick him in the shins, too."

Alete laughed as she got her grandma seated. The older woman picked up her fork but didn't move it toward the cinnamon roll. "Play soccer with me. For old time's sake."

"Old times sake? You mean last month?" The moment Alete had come back from college six years ago and was without a soccer team for the first time in her life since she'd been three, she started a team of adults in Nestled Hollow. Her grandma had been the first member to join and had played with them every week until the balance issue appeared and Parkinson's disease complicated everything, making her too unsteady.

She shrugged. "It feels like forever ago. I miss it. Me, you, the team."

"The entire team misses you. It's not the same having you cheer from the sidelines instead of playing." She couldn't imagine having soccer— and the other sports she played—taken away like Parkinson's had taken them away for her grandma. She could only guess how devastating it was.

"So play with me."

"We'll get you back on the field in no time."

"We better. But play with me now."

"Where? I'm not going to kick the ball to you without you using your walker, and I don't think those wheels are going to appreciate the grass a whole lot."

Her grandma got a mischievous grin on her face as her gaze turned toward the family room. "Your parents won't be home for an hour."

Alete grinned, too, and left her cinnamon roll behind on the table. As her grandma made her way into the family room, using her walker this time, Alete started moving the couches, chairs, and coffee table out of the way.

Once they were against the walls, it left a good amount of space in the middle of the room. She got her grandma's soccer ball from her bedroom and the two of them started kicking it back and forth, with her grandma doing her signature smack-talk with each kick.

Alete might not be able to get the hot fire chief out of her head, nor did she think it was a good idea to kick him in the shins as Ammie suggested, but kicking the soccer ball sure helped relieve the frustration she felt at his words.

ZANE

Zane had spent all day with the three members of his crew who worked over the weekend as they cleaned and inspected the station, vehicles, and equipment. He didn't like getting too close to people or opening up to them, but one thing he loved about being in the fire department was the camaraderie he always had with the guys in the department. The built-in family.

But here, it was feeling anything but friendly. Judah, Liam, and Tila seemed to get along great with each other, but their banter and laughter died down whenever he was around. He hoped it was only a matter of time before they started being more comfortable around each other, but he also knew that being Fire Chief would always put an extra barrier between him and them.

They had just gathered in the small kitchen to start

making dinner when a call came through. The four of them froze as they waited long enough to hear the word "fire," and raced toward their turnouts while the dispatcher finished giving the information.

"Did she just say 132 Proctor?" Liam asked, the color draining from his face.

"Dispatch," Zane said into his radio, "can you please repeat the address?"

"It's Lara Leavitt's house."

Liam's movements kicked into high gear as he pulled on his personal protective equipment. As Zane pulled on his turnouts, he asked Judah, "Who's Lara Leavitt?"

"Liam's sister," Judah said as he shoved his arms into his coat.

Before they'd finished getting their equipment on and climbed into the firetruck, the first of the off-duty firefighters and paramedics came running through the doors and racing to their equipment. Zane barked orders to have Legacy hop in the ambulance with Amy, and Tila, Liam, and Judah to hop into the firetruck with him. Jim came in not long after, and he could see Jarred's car squealing to a stop out front. He instructed them to follow in the side-by-side, and they all left the station, lights blazing.

When they reached Proctor Street, he could see the fire lit up in the night and smoke billowing skyward just a few houses down. When they pulled up to the home and the doors flew open, he instructed Judah to connect the hose to the hydrant, and Tila and Liam to grab hoses.

Liam had put his Nomex hood and face mask on as they neared the street, so he was already racing to the hoses and yanking his off the truck. Zane put a hand on his shoulder. "You can't go in hot. I know this is your sister's house, but you can't help her if you don't stay safe. Don't do anything stupid."

Liam glared at him as he hefted the bulk of the hose in one arm, the end of it in the other, and raced off. As soon as he told Jarred and Jim which direction to head first, he hurried over to the family huddled on the front lawn just as his paramedics reached them. "Is anyone still inside?"

The woman, probably Lara Leavitt, had four young kids and two dogs near her, all grabbing onto each other, coughing from the smoke they'd inhaled. "We all got out."

"Wolfie didn't!" a young boy said. "He's still inside!"

"Is that a dog?" Zane asked.

The woman shook her head. "His stuffed animal." Then she bent down to talk to the boy and Legacy and Amy took over, checking each of them out to see if they needed oxygen or if any of them had burns.

Zane turned his attention back to the fire. With his vantage point and with the communications from each of his guys inside, he was able to direct all of them. He knew his job as the Fire Chief made him the captain of this crew, and with the red helmet came the responsibility to stay outside and direct everyone. But every bit of him felt the wrongness of not being inside with his crew, fighting the fire.

After a few agonizing moments of listening to the noise of the flames as they devoured everything, he heard a scream from one of his guys.

"Report!" He was already pulling on his own Nomex hood, grabbing his face mask, and running toward the house.

"A beam fell on Liam. We're pulling him out."

He reached the house just as they got Liam to the front door. He took over, sliding his arms under Liam's, and dragging him out to the lawn, Amy and Legacy on his heels. Liam disconnected his face mask and tore it off, the pain evident on his face.

"My leg," he said between hissed breaths. "I think it's broken."

Then all four of their heads whipped to the sound of the woman—Liam's sister—shouting, "Paxton? Pax! Where are you?" Her face was frantic, her motions fast and jerky as she ran toward the house, stopping to turn around every few feet, calling her son's name.

Wolfie. Zane instantly knew that the kid had gone back in for his stuffed animal. He ran to the woman and said, "Where's Paxton's bedroom?"

"That one on the end." Her hands flew to her mouth. "I bet he went in through the back door."

Zane secured his face mask and grabbed a pike pole from the truck as he communicated with his guys on the inside and raced around the house to the back door. The fire had started in the kitchen, but the flames had been racing up the walls and across the ceiling.

The floors were squishy, and door frames and parts of the ceiling were crashing down on him as he raced toward the end of the house where the little boy's room was. Several times, he had to use the pike to knock blackened or still burning wood out of his way.

Flames had not yet engulfed the boy's room, but they were licking at the door. Zane threw his shoulder into it and burst inside the room. The little boy, not more than five, was lying on the floor of the smoke-filled room, a gray- and cream-colored stuffed animal clutched in his arms. He didn't move when Zane came in, so he knew the boy was probably unconscious.

Zane dropped the pike pole and scooped him up into his arms, but the flames were already blocking his exit. The turnouts he wore might protect him enough to get back to the outside door if none of the ceiling fell on him, but they wouldn't protect this little guy. He sat him on the ground and used his pike pole to shatter the window, knocking all the sharp glass pieces from the edges, and then handed the boy and his stuffed animal through the window out to the waiting arms of Legacy.

He knew he couldn't get out of the window himself,

with his SCBA tank on his back and with his bulky equipment, but his guys knew what they were doing, and together, they made it out of the burning house.

The ambulance left with the little boy, the boy's family following behind in their own car, and one of the police officers took Liam to the hospital in his patrol car before they got the last of the hot spots extinguished. When Zane and his crew got back to the station, he stayed long enough to pull off his turnouts and didn't even wipe the sweat off his neck before heading to his truck and getting to the hospital as quickly as he could.

He knew he had smears of soot on his face, his NHFD t-shirt was stuck to his sweaty torso, and people could probably smell him from a mile away, but he still had to know the extent of Liam's injury and had to know what happened to the little boy. He went straight through the emergency room and showed his ID to the nurse.

"You're the new fire chief, huh? Sorry to hear about your crew member. Let me take you to his room." As they walked, he asked about the little boy. "Paxton? He inhaled a lot of smoke and will have to stay overnight, but he'll be okay. I heard you saved him."

A whoosh of a relieved breath escaped him.

She opened the curtain to Liam's room where Amy and Legacy stood at his bedside. Liam gave him an exhausted, pained smile.

"Have they told you what you're in for yet?" he asked.

"It's broken. The jury's still out on if it'll need surgery. A boot's definitely in my future."

"What happened in there?"

Liam looked down. "I went in hot, just like you told me not to. And then I was stupid, also like you told me not to be. Ran straight into a room without checking the structure first, and a beam fell on my leg. I'm sorry, Chief. I made a bad mistake, and you can reprimand me or fire me or whatever you have to do. You told me I couldn't help them if I didn't stay safe myself and, well," he met Zane's eyes, "thank you for saving my nephew when I couldn't."

Zane let out a huff of a chuckle and shook his head. "I'd never fire someone who freely admitted their mistakes and wanted to make things right. Although you might find yourself on KP duty when you return until you have that boot off."

Liam smiled and gave him a nod. "That stainless steel will shine good enough to see your reflection when I'm done."

"Have you talked to your sister?"

He shook his head. "Amy did, though."

Zane looked at Amy and was surprised to see that both she and Legacy were looking at him a bit differently. Maybe, just maybe, this was the start of them seeing him as their chief.

"She's shaken up. I mean, obviously. But Paxton's going

to be okay, and she said that's all that matters. Alete Keetch was coming in the room when I was leaving— have you met her? Anyway, I think she was offering to give them a place to stay until everything gets worked out, so at least they'll have a roof over their heads."

Zane left as soon as it seemed right— he wasn't looking to keep stinking up the hospital. So, of course, as he was leaving the room, he nearly bumped into Alete as she was rounding the corner to come in. She was looking maddeningly beautiful, almost like she was doing it to spite him and his current state. She took a big step back, probably to distance herself from the smell of sweat and smoke, and looked him up and down.

"Alete," he said, giving her a nod.

"Zane. I'm sorry to hear about the man down. Good job saving Pax, though."

"Thanks," he said, then turned and left as quickly as he could get out of there.

ALETE

lete stepped into the produce section, basket in hand, on a mission to find a few perfect avocados. She was having friends over for games, and even though Morgan had shown up late for work, making Alete stay longer than she'd planned, she was still determined to make her famous guacamole.

She found three that, when given a gentle squeeze, were perfectly ripe and the perfect color. In a hurry to get everything else she needed, she spun around toward the cilantro right as the person behind her turned toward her, and they bumped into each other.

"Oh, sorry! I didn't...Oh. Zane."

"Alete."

Not the person she wanted to see right now. Even though seeing an attractive firefighter with a grocery cart, shopping for food for the crew on staff for the weekend was something she could've stuck around to watch for hours, especially after having seen him at the hospital. But she still hadn't gotten over the Business Alliance meeting that he had crashed with his arrogant plans.

At least he didn't seem any happier to see her than she was to see him. He turned to the apple display he'd been headed to, so she brushed him off, too, and started looking for the perfect bunch of cilantro. Once she found it and moved to find a single crisp jalapeno, she heard Zane clear his throat right behind her. She turned to face him.

"This probably won't be the last time we bump into each other, will it?"

Alete picked up an onion and gave it a squeeze to see how firm it was. "Nope. Small town." Normally, it was one of the perks. With Zane, though, it felt very much the opposite.

He reached a hand up and rubbed the back of his neck. Was he nervous? Uncomfortable? Whatever it was, it was kind of adorable on him. Adorable and annoying, but mostly because it was the man trying to take over without even knowing anything about what he was proposing.

"Listen," he said. "We're both professionals. We shouldn't let getting off on the wrong foot make things awkward for all our future bumping into each other experiences. Can we maybe start over?"

Alete hesitated for a brief moment then nodded. They were likely going to see each other, and she hated having unresolved things between her and others. She would much rather they work things out. "I'd like that."

"I'm a bit passionate about this town being safe and protected, so I came across a bit too strongly in that meeting. I apologize."

Alete wondered what might've happened in his life that would make him so passionate about protecting a town he knew nothing about and hadn't even stepped foot in until a few days ago, and she wished she knew him well enough to ask. "Well, some might say that I'm a bit passionate about taking care of this town, too. So I, also, apologize for coming off so strongly."

He gave a quick nod like everything was settled. She hoped it was, but it did seem a bit too easy. After all, they had only apologized for how strongly they presented their side—not for believing in their side.

Zane drummed his fingers on the handle of the cart. Clearly, he had more he wanted to say besides an apology. "There's a lot that needs to happen to keep this town safe, and some of those things cost quite a bit. I've applied for grants and I'm fairly confident we'll get a good chunk of it that way. I've worked with the county and state emergency management departments, and have gotten all I can from them. But it's going to take more than that."

She put the onion in her basket and moved down to

the limes and picked one up. "I get it. I do. I run a business, and there's never enough money for all the things that beg for it. Figuring out what areas need it the most can be quite the juggling act."

She hoped he got the underlying message— that just because something needed money, didn't mean it should get it. It was all a matter of figuring out what was needed first and not spending more than the budget contained. If he couldn't get all the things he wanted with the funds he had, some things were going to have to wait.

"Exactly," he said, relief evident in his voice. "Sometimes you have an area in your business that might be very deserving of having money dedicated to it, but you can't, because it's needed somewhere else even more. It doesn't mean you can't spend money on that area in the future—just that you can't right now."

She nodded, thinking they were on the same page until he kept talking.

"That's exactly what I was proposing by cutting the town celebrations for a while. Taking money from somewhere that might be deserving of it and giving it to a need that is more pressing."

She wasn't going to fault him for not knowing how this town worked— he hadn't been here long. But she wasn't about to let him stay in the dark, either. If building community was a religion, she was the preacher. If it was a class, she was the professor. If it was a nation, she was the president.

"It's *not* more pressing. I get why it might look that way on paper, but knowing the town from the inside out, I'll tell you that those things that you're thinking don't matter to this town's wellbeing actually matter a lot."

"I bet there are a good number of people who feel the same. On a scale of one to ten, I'm sure the town celebrations are probably a ten."

Alete narrowed her eyes and crossed her arms as best as she could with a basket hanging from one arm. Could he not even at least try to say that as if he believed it even a little tiny bit? She knew a placating voice when she heard one.

"I'm just saying that other things are needed more right now," he said. "I mean, if you've got something that's a ten and you've got money in the town budget, then go ahead and spend it on the ten. But what I need the money for isn't simply a ten. It's a one hundred. And when you've got something ranking one hundred, a ten doesn't really matter."

Alete ground her teeth. *Doesn't really matter.* Three days he'd been in town, and already he was arrogant enough to think he knew where each item would rank. She was glad he had checked out of the inn this morning to move into his own apartment, if for no other reason than to have fewer chances to bump into him.

She definitely didn't trust any words that would come out of her mouth right now to be "professional" or coming anywhere close to smoothing things over between them. So she just said a clipped, "Good luck with your one hundred, Zane," and turned and strode up to the cash registers, ignoring the look of bewilderment on the man's face.

seven

ZANE

Zane pulled out another dust-covered box from the wall of storage closets along the side of the fire station and found another emergency frequency radio inside. He was three hours into the job of searching through years and years of forgotten equipment, but as far as a radio was concerned, they could still work with the old stuff.

The job involved a lot of heaving and hefting box upon box, but he was still frustrated when he'd arrived at work today about how off track Alete had taken the meeting, so he figured it would help to throw some aggression at the mess.

It turned out that he only had staff on duty at the fire station from noon on Fridays to noon on Sundays, and the rest of the week his crew was only on call. So he was there by himself, finding all the things he could, Ranger at his side.

When the dog started barking his "someone's coming" bark, Zane hit his head on the ceiling of the small space and cursed as he stepped out into the bay.

"You know," Stockton said as he eyed the neat piles of equipment spread across two portable tables, "if you would have told me you were doing this today, I'd have come in earlier to help."

"When you agreed to hold off your official retirement for two weeks and come in for a couple of hours a day, I doubt this was the work you had in mind." Stockton was being decent to him; the least he could do was to return the favor.

But the man stepped in and helped anyway.

As the two men worked, thoughts of the meeting and Alete's part in it, and of running into her at the hospital and at the grocery store, ran through his mind again— like it had half a dozen times already that day— causing a fresh wave of frustration to wash over him. And every time it did, he swore the irritation got stronger. Maybe he just needed to get it out.

He set a partial roll of dusty duct tape on the table with a little more force than he'd intended. "She just doesn't understand what I'm trying to do here."

Stockton looked up from the box he was crouched next to. "Who? Alete?"

He gave a single nod. "She doesn't get the big picture. If she did, she would see that I'm trying to *help* her beloved town. She acts like I'm some demon who's blown into town, ready to destroy everything."

It didn't help that she was so attractive, with her soft face, her fiery eyes, that long athletic build, and her beautiful neck. Had he ever even noticed a woman's neck before? What was he doing noticing hers, when she was obviously out to make his life difficult? The whole thing was maddening.

He walked over to the storage cubby and grabbed another box, then thumped it down on the table. "And it doesn't matter that she isn't on the city council or running the business alliance or any other position with an official title. Did you see the way everyone else in the room reacted? That woman has more power than any of them, and she's using it to sway everyone against me. It's like she's out to destroy any hope this town has of becoming prepared. She's infuriating."

Why was he even wasting his time here?

He shook his head as he opened the box. He was here because Nestled Hollow needed him, even if Alete couldn't see it. And because he wouldn't quit on a town.

"You know," Stockton said, "if one side of the coin is irritation and annoyance, they say that the other side of that same coin is love."

He narrowed his eyes at Stockton and then tossed a

broken helmet into the garbage can, making a *thud*. "Well, that's the thing about coins. You can only see one side at a time, so I think it's safe to say that there will never be any feelings of love coming from me."

Stockton just chuckled, which made it all the more maddening.

Whatever Zane had thought about the intriguing woman on the ladder five nights ago when he'd checked into his hotel was wrong. She was a menace. A boat rocker. And on top of that, she had gotten him to say— in front of the entire Main Street Business Alliance and the City Council, no less— his thoughts about people showing love by protecting you. He hadn't meant to get that personal.

He found another radio in the box and added it to the table. There might very well be more hidden somewhere in this hidden mess, but even if there wasn't, this was enough. He picked one up. "I'm going to find some interested people in this town, and start a ham radio group. We'll meet every week at first, get everyone trained, do some emergency checks, and move it to a monthly meeting when they've all got it down. And," he said, pointing at Stockton with the radio, "I'm going to do it with or without Little Miss Town Celebration's approval."

He put the radio back down and looked at the stack of them with his hands on his hips. "I'll just keep her out of the loop as much as possible. I figure if I can stay far from her, I can actually run things as I planned."

"Sounds like a good idea," Stockton said.

But, as Zane was learning was Stockton's usual, the man had more brewing in his thoughts than what he said, and they'd stay there unless someone pulled them out. But he wasn't going to work to pull them out today. Instead, he just nodded.

As Zane sorted through the next box, pulling out anything of value and placing each in its spot on the tables, and tossing most of it in the giant trash can that was now mostly full, his phone sounded its tone for texts. He pulled it out of its case on his belt and looked at the screen. "It's the mayor," he told Stockton. "He wants to meet with me in five." Good. He could tell him his new plan.

"About that coin," Stockton called out as Zane headed toward the front door, "you know it was made to be flipped!"

———

The city building was small but still stood important at the end of Main Street, in the way only a small building in a small town could. Zane had left Ranger with Stockton and walked kitty-corner from the fire station to City Hall, and went in through the front door. It was where he'd had his interview a few weeks ago, so he was familiar with the lobby, which he was sure had been decorated by the big-haired receptionist at the front desk.

"Well, hello, Mr. Collins—or I guess I should call you Chief Collins now. It's so great to see you again! How are you liking our little town?"

"Hello, Gloria," he said, grateful for her nameplate because he'd forgotten it since the last time he'd been in. "It's a fine place you've got here." He eyed the conference room where he'd had his interview, wondering if that was where he'd be meeting Mayor Stone.

"And it's full of fine people. Speaking of which, now, I wasn't at the meeting yesterday, of course, but I heard that you and Alete have quite the chemistry!"

He gave her a tight smile and hoped that that rumor hadn't passed far. He was there to do a job—to get an emergency preparedness plan set in place for Nestled Hollow, and then to move on. He knew how much time and focus that took and how little free time he'd have. He had come here with zero intentions of dating, and now that he had spent some time with Alete, he knew she was the last person in the whole town he wanted to spend any time with. "Well, you know the way chemistry is. Sometimes you put two chemicals together, and you get an explosion that can take out everyone around."

She laughed and playfully swatted at him, hitting nothing but air. "You are so funny! Frank and I need to have you over for pie sometime. Welcome you to town and all."

He hoped she hadn't noticed the creased brow of confusion he knew hit his face for a small moment. Why would this woman want him over for pie? This wasn't flirting. Did she think he could do something for her? He gave the most non-committal "Yeah, sure" he could, then said, "I have a meeting with Mayor Stone I need to get to."

"His office is right there, honey," Gloria said, pointing to an office on the opposite side of the lobby from the conference room.

He walked into an office that was decently large for the size of the building. The bookshelves and end tables along the far wall, as well as the desk that the mayor sat behind, were all filled with enough books and papers and trinkets that could only accumulate over years and years. Maybe decades. The mayor immediately stood, walked around his desk, and shook his hand. "Thanks for coming, Zane."

Instead of sitting down at the round table pushed into the corner, the mayor leaned against it, so Zane leaned against the mayor's desk. "I'm glad you asked me here. I've got a lot I'd like to talk to you about. I emailed you my detailed plan early this morning."

"I got it. Thank you."

"As I've been working today, I've been thinking. The

plan will go much better with the support of the business owners in the city. After experiencing the Main Street Business Alliance meeting yesterday, I realize that route had been a mistake. I figure that between the two of us, we could just go from business to business and meet with them individually. If we could just shut Alete Keetch out of all parts of it, I think—"

"That's actually what I wanted to talk to you about," Mayor Stone said.

"Good." Zane relaxed into the desk he leaned against.

The mayor scratched his cheek. "I think the two of you should work together."

"What?" Zane sat up straight, alarm and confusion warring for dominance. "In what way could that possibly make sense? Mayor, that woman is a menace. Didn't you get from the meeting that she wants to undermine everything I do?"

"I've looked over your plans, Chief. The ones you sent before you arrived and the ones you sent this morning. You know me and the city council are behind you. I think where you're taking our town is good. I believe in what you're trying to do."

"Then why propose that I work with Alete? She's got a hotel to run. I'm sure she's a very busy woman."

"And I'm sure she would make time. Chief, you're an expert at so many aspects of getting us prepared. It's working with the people of this town, specifically, that you aren't an expert at. She is."

This was not something he signed on for. But his position as Emergency Management Director was under the city manager, which just happened to be Mayor Stone. His position as Fire Chief was under the mayor, which was also Mayor Stone. So with both of his job titles, he reported to the same man. He didn't feel like he should just throw around demands, especially when all he needed was to appeal to the mayor's sense of logic.

"A disaster could hit at any time," Zane said. "But with that burn scar on the mountain, you know as well as I do that come spring, this town *will* be in an emergency situation and we need to be prepared. How big of an emergency is yet to be determined, but there are a lot of things we can control to make sure it's not as bad, and we can prepare for the things we can't control. That puts us on a narrow timeline to get everything done. Working with Alete will slow it all down. I'd get nowhere."

"If you *don't* work with her, I worry you'll get nowhere."

Zane stood up and turned around, facing the painting on the wall of Main Street in what was probably the seventies, running his hand through his hair. He turned back to Mayor Stone. "For the bulk of my time spent in emergency management in Springvale, outside of working with the Emergency Management Director, I worked with the city manager and the fire department. Surely I just need to work with my crew and you."

"And you will work with me. But you don't understand small-town dynamics, son. It's not about making plans and then executing those plans. It takes people. You're new, so I don't expect you to know our town. But you'll need to if you want to make headway."

"Okay, okay. I get where you're coming from. But she's not the only person who knows this town well. Surely there's someone other than her who I can work with."

"And accomplish the big plans you want to accomplish? And in the small amount of time you're proposing? I'm not sure there is."

Zane ground his teeth.

"You seem like the kind of guy who doesn't like to do things part way. You do things one hundred percent, the best they can be, or not at all. Am I right?"

Zane gave a single curt nod.

"There's only one way you're going to get everything you want, and that's if you work with Alete. Oh! I hear her out with Gloria now. Right on time."

As Mayor Stone walked out to the lobby, Zane crossed his arms and looked out the window, knowing he was about to be ambushed. He stared at the small grassy playground as the mayor and Alete exchanged friendly greetings. She asked how his wife and kids were, calling them each by name as if she wanted to show off how much she knew that he didn't.

When they finally headed toward Mayor Stone's office, Alete walked through the door first, her face lit up with a smile that would've been downright intoxicating if it hadn't been on her. As soon as she saw him in the room, though, the smile fell and she narrowed her eyes. "What is *he* doing here?" She turned like maybe she was the one being ambushed, but Mayor Stone was walking in right behind her, blocking her exit.

"Now, neither of you needs to be hostile. I want to propose something that will benefit both of you in the end."

Alete glared at him, arms crossed, unmoving, for several long moments before she let out a huge breath, took two steps forward, and dropped into one of the chairs at the table. "Propose away."

Mayor Stone nodded, and then took a seat at the table, too. Zane stayed standing, leaning against the mayor's desk.

Alete didn't interrupt the mayor as often as he had while the man told her how he thought they should work together. It was like she was always trying to one-up him on everything. When the mayor asked if she was willing to work with Zane, he looked out the window instead of watching to see what kind of emotions crossed her face. He could guess without looking.

"I love this town, and I agree that it is important to get an emergency plan in place for our city. But Chief Collins—" she emphasized the name, like calling him Zane was something only friends would do, and she was showing that they were anything but, "—doesn't care about the town. He only cares about the end result. Getting the job done, not *how* he gets it done. He just wants to come in and conquer and destroy, not caring about what he's destroying, as long as he can get his precious end result."

How could she not understand that caring about the end result *did* show that he cared about the town? People didn't protect people they didn't care about. She just couldn't see past her own way of doing things. But doing this job without the mayor's cooperation was impossible. If it weren't for the fact that he'd likely lose that without agreeing to work with this infuriating woman, he'd walk out the door right now.

"And that," Mayor Stone said, raising an eyebrow at her pointedly, "is exactly why he needs you to work with him on it."

Zane stood and strode back to the window, looking out of it instead of at them. He knew how to do his job, and he knew how to do it well. He did *not* need a babysitter. The best outcome he could hope for right now would be for her to say no to the mayor.

Alete let out a long, slow breath, and even without

looking at her, he knew by the sound of it that she was probably going to say yes in the end. "How much time will I have to spend with him?"

Zane turned around. "There's a lot to do, so it's guaranteed to take time away from your town cheerleader duties."

He knew he was a jerk for saying it, but he didn't back down. Instead, the two of them stared each other down, neither flinching.

Then Alete shifted her gaze to Mayor Stone as she stood up and held out her hand to shake his. "Thank you so much for the offer, Mayor, but it's just not going to work for me."

Turning on her heel in very purposeful motions that gave away just how angry she was, even if her face showed nothing, Alete walked out the door.

Good riddance.

Mayor Stone turned toward Zane. He figured the mayor would chew him out for not doing more to help talk Alete into helping and making comments that made her not want to help, but he didn't. Instead, the mayor let out a long, slow, defeated breath. He offered his hand, and Zane shook it. "Good luck, Chief. Here's hoping you can pull off a miracle."

Challenge accepted. Without Alete trying to stop all forward progress, that was exactly what he planned to do.

eight

ALETE

Alete called in her whole team, keeping the soccer ball bouncing on her foot as everyone gathered. She was the unofficial coach, mostly because she had played in college and because she was the one who started their informal team. It consisted of every adult in Nestled Hollow, regardless of age, that she could talk into playing.

She always ran some drills with them to get warmed up and to help up their game, and then they drew sticks to divide them into two teams. They played a game no matter how many people showed up. Occasionally it was as few as three on three, and a couple of times it was 15 on 15— a great big melee on the field. But usually, it was somewhere in the middle.

Today there were fourteen of them— a nice even number, so she counted out seven dowels with a green end and seven with a purple end, mixed them all together, and then held them out into the middle of their circle, the colored side hidden in her hand.

"Yes! I'm a Gator!" Aaron said as he pulled out a stick with a green end, then grabbed one of the green mesh pinny jerseys and pulled it over his head. He had joined the team shortly after he and Alete's friend Macie got engaged over Christmas. He hadn't played much soccer before, but he had been an Olympic swimmer and was one of the fiercest competitors they had. Alete loved being on the team opposite him. Aaron's eyes landed on Macie, who was now his new wife. She held up her purple-tipped stick, and his face fell. "We aren't teammates?"

Macie shook her head. "I'm a Crusher."

"But we got on the same team," Whitney said as Eli handed her a green jersey. She rose up on her toes and gave him a quick kiss, and they grinned sickeningly sweet at each other, her wedding ring shining like it had been the one to get the part of the tooth in a toothpaste commercial.

Alete shook her head. At least Nate wasn't here with Tory, or there might have been some kind of explosion of recently married, elated couples. Brooke and Cole only came to about one-third of the games— they weren't among the fourteen today either, or they would've added their own engaged-to-be-married fuel to the explosion, and then there would be more kissing on the field than playing.

"Come on, people," Alete said as she pulled her own green jersey over her head. "We're here to play!"

The fans on the sidelines cheered as the fourteen players took the field. They didn't draw a big crowd—mostly the kids of any parents who were playing, and now, her grandma. If any adults came to watch, she was usually pretty successful at getting them to play instead.

"Go Gators," her grandma yelled loudly. She was the one who had named their teams when they first got the pinnies, and she liked to shout the names every chance she got.

To start the game, Aaron kicked the ball just barely over the line and to the side where she could get it. She used all the footwork her middle school, high school, and college coaches had drilled into her, successfully keeping it away from Macie. The girl might look like a strong wind could blow her over, but she was fierce. She passed the ball to Whitney and Whitney kicked hard to make the goal, but Tory caught it and goalie-kicked it in a high arc across the field.

The ball was coming down right at Candace, their newest player who was still a little afraid of the ball. She ducked, looking down, her hands on top of her head to protect it when the ball hit her right on the hands.

The game was informal enough that they didn't use a

ref. Her grandma was so used to being the most vocal player ref, and now that she was sidelined, she even brought a whistle. She immediately blew it. "Hands! But the penalty is wiped clean because it was also one beautiful head shot! Plus, that duck was rather graceful. Way to go, Candace!"

Alete chuckled and the players kept going as if the whistle had never been blown. It broke her heart that her grandma wasn't on the field, too, at least until this new medication kicked in, but hearing her typical refereeing made it feel more right. Alete got the ball back and drove it down the field, but Macie managed to get it away from her.

"Come on, Alete," her grandma yelled. "Get that ball back and kick it like it's the new fire chief's plans for this town!"

"Ammie!"

"What kind of a kick was that, Carl?" her grandma said, acting like she hadn't even heard Alete's rebuke. "Don't you make me come out there in my walker to show you how it's done." She blew her whistle. "Out of bounds. Crushers' ball."

For the two teams being chosen completely by chance, they ended up being pretty even, which wasn't always the case. Both sides had some newer players, and both had some very competitive ones.

Between Macie's defense and Tory's ability to stop

every ball that even neared the goal, they had shut Alete down a little too effectively. When she got the ball again, she took it up the left side instead of the right, hoping to avoid Macie, and instead was challenged by her grandma's friend, Martha Ellen, or "Boots," as Grandma called her.

The two of them were bumping shoulders and both going for the ball, but Alete kept control of it. Then, just as she got the ball turned away from Martha Ellen, the woman grabbed her jersey to stop her. "Holding!" Alete called out right as her grandma blew the whistle.

"Penalty on the Gators for pushing Boots!"

"Ammie! I didn't push."

"Ahh, but you forget," she said, holding up the lanyard that held the whistle and giving it a shake. "I hold the whistle and, therefore, the power."

Alete shook her head as she smiled at her grandma. "Oh, I see. You show preference to someone you share a birth decade with over someone you share blood with. Fair enough."

Martha Ellen did a little dance right before she ran to kick the penalty shot.

Even with her grandma's cheering and crazy referee calls, Alete was losing steam in the last five minutes after battling it out all game against Macie. When she got the ball again and was driving it down the field, her grandma called out, "Come on! Look alive out there! Think of Zane with a giant blow torch, crispifying all those town celebrations, and funnel all those emotions into making a goal!"

But before she could shoot, Macie got the ball away from her.

"Really?" her grandma called out. "That comment didn't get you the goal?"

Honestly, the comment distracted her from the game. She still felt guilty that she told Mayor Stone that she wouldn't help Zane last week. She easily could have helped. She was willing to do pretty much anything for her town, and the mayor was a great guy, so she would've had no problem telling him yes.

But Zane was just so arrogant and was willing to sacrifice anything in pursuit of his goal, not even caring enough to find out if those things had importance first. And that showed he didn't care about people. *Her* people.

She was distracted enough that the Crushers even scored a goal. As they took their places at the center to kick-off, Whitney took Aaron's pass and dribbled it down the field. As she neared the goal, Tory moved forward in anticipation of Whitney's shot. But instead of shooting, Whitney passed it to Alete, and she was wide open. She could almost feel her goal-scoring kick as the ball came to her.

But then her grandma yelled, "Imagine that Zane is here on the sidelines, looking smokin' hot, wearing a t-shirt stretched tight across those chest muscles, cheering for you to make the goal!"

So completely distracted by her grandma's shouts, she stepped wrong, slid, and then somehow managed to both kick the ball straight up into the air and kick both legs out from under her, coming down hard on her back. A moment later, the ball came back down and hit her in the stomach, knocking the small amount of breath that she'd managed to suck in right back out of her.

She lay on the ground, telling the circle of players that gathered around her that she was fine, and imagined how red her face was. Between the embarrassment at that shot and the force of her resulting fall, along with the embarrassment at how much it had affected her to imagine Zane cheering her on in a tight t-shirt, she was pretty sure she was beet red.

She heard the clicking of her grandma's walker as she lifted it and then set it back down with each step as she neared. Then the circle of teammates made a hole big enough for her grandma and her walker. Ammie leaned over the walker, looking down at her. "Sweetheart. That comment was supposed to make you play better, not make you forget how legs worked."

Alete chuckled and pushed herself to a sitting position, then grabbed hold of Eli's hand when he offered it and let him pull her to standing.

——————

After the game, she and her grandma headed to With a Cherry on Top for their usual post-game analysis and ice cream. As they dissected her performance, how the teams did, and Ammie's refereeing and smack-talking, she noticed her grandma looking sadder and sadder when that was the part that usually made her most excited.

"Let's talk about something else," she suggested.

Her grandma let out a big exhale and threw her arms on the table. "I just want to play again!"

"Do you think the medicine the doctor gave you is helping the Parkinson's at all?"

Ammie shook her head. "No. If I can't get rid of either my balance problems or the stiffness when I walk, I can't be without my blasted walker. And I just met with my ENT, and he said this lack of balance is likely here to stay.
"

"I am so sorry." Alete reached across the table and gave her grandma's hand a squeeze.

Ammie took a big bite of her Nestled Hollow Heaven, and as soon as she swallowed said, "But I tell you what. I meet with my Parkinson's doc in two weeks, and I'm going to have him sign me up for that deep brain stimulation surgery. Then I can kick that walker in the shins—" she shot a glare at the walker, "—and I'll be back to playing soccer again in no time."

"That sounds exciting, Ammie. I'm happy for you."

Her grandma grinned and savored the last two bites of her ice cream. As they were heading back out to the car, she said, "But since you offered the change in subjects, let's talk about your love life. Or lack of it."

Alete groaned as she opened the car door for Ammie. She loved her grandma and didn't want her dwelling on what she couldn't do, and that was the only reason why she was willing to endure this conversation.

As they drove back to Alete's parents' house to take her grandma home, Ammie said, "You know, I've heard there are dating apps you can get right on your phone. You just put in your picture and some information about yourself and you'll practically have guys beating down your door."

Why, oh why, was the mental image that popped into her mind at her grandma's words an image of Zane knocking at her door? And of course, since her grandma had planted the thought, he was wearing a t-shirt that stretched across his chest muscles. And his short hair was still perfectly mussed as if it was begging fingers to be run through it. Of course, in her mental image, he wasn't trying to destroy town traditions. He was just smiling mischievously.

"Ammie, I'm not getting a dating app."

"Is it because you don't like to toot your own horn? I

can write up the bio for you. It'll be a hoot and the guys will be lining up to date you."

"*No!* Seriously, Ammie, I'm just not looking to date." She pulled into the driveway and put the car into park, banishing thoughts of Zane. Not that she minded dating. It was the getting serious she didn't like.

Back when she was nineteen and had stars in her eyes, she fell in love and got engaged with a dreamy guy she could totally picture growing old with, hand-in-hand. She had seen how great her parents' marriage was and had wanted the same thing for herself. They didn't argue and she'd known that she'd have to change in order to have a relationship like they had, so she had. She'd been the most agreeable, most amenable she'd been her entire life. She'd poured everything into making that relationship with Josh work.

But two things had happened. Since she had become such an agreeable doormat, Josh totally took advantage of it and constantly bulldozed her. She found out he had been cheating on her the whole time and he'd been lying about other things, too. Josh had been thrilled with their relationship— he had someone who would be nice and understanding and assume the best no matter what he did. He may have loved the relationship, but it had been slowly crushing her.

The second thing didn't happen until a couple of months before they were supposed to get married. She and her mom were meeting with the caterer to decide on the menu for the rehearsal dinner— without Josh, who had been busy with work—and she couldn't decide what food to have and left crying.

It had seemed like such a stupid reason for a meltdown, but it hadn't been about the food. As she'd been looking over menus, it had suddenly struck her how much she didn't like the person she had made herself become to fit the marriage. She didn't even enjoy being alone with herself, and she knew she didn't want to go through life like that.

It wasn't much longer before she confirmed the cheating and lying that she had suspected all along but had never allowed to take front and center in her thoughts. She stood straight and tall, summoned the inner Aleteness she knew she had and called everything off. It had been the moment when she'd felt the most like herself in a full year.

She wasn't willing to be a doormat, but she also didn't want to fight her way through a marriage. She'd decided then and there that she was never going to change who she was in order to meet someone else's expectations, even if that meant that she couldn't ever have the dreamy guy with the storybook marriage like her parents did.

"I like my independence. I like to do what I want when I want, and not have anyone interfere with that. You, of all people, Ammie, understand that. I know you do." She got out of the car and grabbed the walker from the trunk, then opened up her grandma's door and gave her a hand out of her seat.

"Oh, I like my independence just as fiercely as you do. But I also *really* liked being married to my Frank." She gave a happy sigh as she grabbed hold of Alete's arm that wasn't holding the walker and they walked toward the kitchen door at the side of the house. "Your grandpa was just so thoughtful. And at night, after we got the kids in bed, he would come into our bedroom singing *Love Me Tender* in his deepest voice and wearing nothing but—"

"Stop! Ammie, I beg you not to finish that sentence."

Her grandma smiled and shrugged. "I'm just saying that there are benefits to not staying single forever."

As they neared the door, they saw her parents in the backyard. The two of them were working together to weed a section of the flower garden with their backs toward Alete. Her dad was shoveling by a weed whose roots must've gone way down, and her mom looked up from where she was kneeling, pulling weeds. "Do you know what I was thinking about today?"

Most people would just ask 'What?' to be polite. But not her parents. Her dad looked at her mom and asked, "That since precipitation, evaporation, and condensation is a closed cycle, the water we're using today has been around for as long as the Earth has existed?"

"Yes! That's it exactly!"

And then the two of them went on to discuss theories of where the water they just used in the garden had been "in its younger years" as they worked.

Her grandma chuckled beside her. "Those crazy kids. They're always so in sync."

Alete opened the kitchen door and helped her grandma up the two stairs leading into the house, then set her walker down in the kitchen. She motioned in the general direction of her parents. "See why I can't ever get married?"

At her grandma's confused look, she said, "They don't even need to talk, because they already know what each other is going to say. They just talk for fun. They do everything together just because they like being around each other so much and they're always looking out for each other. It's like they know through telepathy when one has a sore muscle that needs to be rubbed or when one has a craving for nachos on a Tuesday night and they automatically fill that need."

When her grandma sat down at the table, Alete did, too.

"I mean, I've lived with one of the best examples of marriage that there is. My parents are about as perfect for one another as a couple can get, and do you know how rare that is? The chance of me finding someone I wouldn't argue with all the time is so low they're practically nonexistent." She glanced out the kitchen window at them. "But how could I settle for anything less after growing up seeing how it could be?"

"You're right," her grandma said. "Your parents have ruined any chance you have of a happy future."

She rolled her eyes at her grandma's sarcasm which she somehow always seemed to pull off without the slightest bit of sarcasm in her voice.

All three of her siblings had taken her parents' marriage as proof that it could work, and they made it happen. But she couldn't do the same. She knew how ridiculous it sounded, but that didn't make the fear any less real, less huge, or less likely to keep her up at night.

She had seen enough relationships where both parties got on each other's nerves to know it wasn't something she was interested in. And she knew was as headstrong as she was, she wasn't going to back down from many fights. If she ever got married, her relationship with her husband would never be as harmonious as her parents' relationship.

Nope. It didn't matter if someone she was inexplicably drawn to wore a t-shirt that stretched across his muscles or not. She would gladly stay single forever.

nine

ZANE

Zane walked further down the bay as he and his crew moved in their effort to wash the big fire truck. He had found that with this group, keeping them busy during their All Crew meetings actually helped. They had already discussed the calls they'd had since the last meeting— a couple of search-and-rescues, some EMT calls, and even a kitten stuck in a tree, which he thought people only called fire departments for back in *Leave it to Beaver* days. He looked down at his clipboard for the next item on his agenda.

"Jim, how did the last meeting with the radio team go?"

A couple of weeks ago, Stockton had suggested that Zane go to the Nestled Hollow Gazette to announce that they were looking to form a ham radio group. He had thought it would be pointless, because who actually read physical newspapers anymore? By their circulation numbers, apparently something like 95% of this town, which was insane. The woman who ran the paper, Whitney, not only easily agreed to include the article, but wrote it up for him and put it on the front page.

Eight guys—five older folks, one younger guy, and one older married couple showed up at their first meeting.

He found out that Jim, the oldest guy in the department, was already a radio geek and was thrilled to start a group of people who were going to take part in his favorite hobby. Jim seemed to have the group so under control that Zane knew he could spend his time elsewhere.

Jim held both thumbs up. "Coming right along. I'll have them trained in everything on the list you gave me in no time."

Zane scribbled some notes on his paper and then looked up when he heard a squeal. Judah, one of the youngest in the department, had been rinsing the soap off one area of the firetruck and was now spraying Jarred. Jarred responded by throwing his big soapy sponge right at Judah's chest. The two were grinning so much that he knew that they were only moments away from a water fight that would pull in all of his crew and would probably get Liam's boot that was protecting his injured leg wet.

"Guys! Quit horsing around. We're having a meeting here."

Jarred picked up his sponge and Judah went back to rinsing the side of the truck, but he didn't miss Liam's mumbled, "Chief Stockton wouldn't have told us to quit horsing around."

Zane growled softly. When were they going to understand that he and Stockton were not the same and to quit comparing them?

"Getting back on track, I heard from Principal Ploeger at the elementary. He sent home instructions with all the kids to make a family emergency plan and decide where they were going to meet in each scenario and do a fire drill in their own homes. He asked them to bring back a signed form when they did, saying their family had completed it. He just reported that they got ninety percent of the forms back."

All of his crew cheered. Zane was still shaking his head that the principal managed to get a response like that. Apparently, if he offered to wear pajamas to school the next day *and* let the beloved lunch lady shave his head bald — in his pajamas and during an assembly— kids got on board.

"When is he shaving his head?" Legacy, the young EMT, asked.

Zane looked down at his paper. "On Thursday."

Legacy turned to Jarred. "We should offer to let the

principal shave our heads at the assembly, too." Then he turned to Zane. "Can we, Chief?"

"Sure. Go for it."

"All of us?" Jarred asked.

"I'm in," Judah and Liam said at the same time.

"Not me," Amy said, tossing her braid over her shoulder. "And don't you even think of coming up from behind me with scissors, Liam, or you'll find yourself on the floor, wondering what hit you. The same goes for my girl, Tila." She put a soapy arm around Tila's shoulder.

"I don't know," Tila said, running her hand through her shoulder-length hair. "Maybe I can get this side shaved."

Zane shook his head. This crew was good in emergency situations—he'd already seen them in action for a few rescues. Maybe there was no way to keep them focused in the absence of imminent danger.

He looked down at the next item on his list, but before he opened his mouth to speak, Stockton came walking into the bay. The man was officially retired now, but he kept coming back just as much as he had been at the start. Maybe Zane should just start assigning him duties.

Zane said hello to Stockton at the same time the rest of his crew said, "Hello, Chief!" They had the guy's retirement party already, yet they were still calling him Chief. He gave up hoping the transition would be smoother. Although maybe "Chief" had all but become the man's name. Most of the town showed up to the retirement party, and all of them called Stockton "Chief."

Alete had been there, too, talking to everyone, looking amazing in a deep blue dress. As he watched her, he decided that she wasn't the town cheerleader. She was more like someone running for Student Body President and was trying to get every student's vote.

Except his.

She was cordial enough, but he could see the fire in those fierce eyes. She still greeted him and acted nice, pretending like she hadn't walked out of the meeting where Mayor Stone asked her to help him. But also pretending that he hadn't been the jerk who prompted her walk-out. The woman was just so infuriating that he couldn't stop thinking about her.

And here he was, getting just as distracted as his crew was.

"Okay, next item," he said, and his crew stopped chatting and glanced his way while they worked. "We need neighborhood preparedness coordinators. I went to Whitney at the Gazette and had her write an article asking for volunteers. I was hoping that we would get enough of a response that we could pick and choose who we thought were the most capable and responsible, but we haven't gotten a single taker."

After the response they'd had for the ham radio group, he thought this part would be easy. He was still baffled that no one had applied. He got the newspaper delivered to his new apartment, so he'd been able to read the article, and he'd thought it was great.

"If any of you have suggestions beyond going door-to-door talking to people, I'd love to hear them."

No one answered for a few moments until Legacy spoke up. "There's a giant town map in the conference room at City Hall. It has everyone's names listed on their houses. Maybe we can just go through the list and see."

Zane had seen the map when he'd interviewed for the job. He pictured it and imagined how it would go with the eight— or nine, with Stockton— of them gathered around it, reading off each name and discussing. This was a small town, but not *that* small. "If this were a town of a hundred adults, I could see that working. That can be our last resort plan. Any other suggestions?"

No one immediately raised their hand, so Zane said, "Stockton? Do you have any suggestions?"

The guy raised an eyebrow in a "you already know my suggestion" kind of way, then gave a sly smile and said, "All you need to do is flip the coin."

His crew likely had no idea what Stockton's cryptic response meant. So Zane responded with something equally cryptic. "The coin is firmly staying at irritation side up." He didn't need Stockton telling him that he needed to work with Alete, too. Things had been going great without her.

Amy raised her hand, so Zane nodded at her. "What about asking Alete Keetch to help? She knows everybody, and she can convince anyone to do practically anything. I bet she'd know who to ask."

Everyone nodded and chatted about what a great idea that was.

He drew in a slow, deep breath, feeling his jaw clenching. "Any *other* ideas?"

Jarred slowly and sheepishly raised his hand, which made Zane not want to call on the guy, but he did anyway. "No other ideas, but I just wanted to say that my grandma Misty wants to have you over for ice cream sometime. You know, to say hi."

This was his seventh offer to go to someone's house for dessert, and, knowing this town, probably sitting on chairs on their porch and shooting the breeze. He still didn't get it.

"Noted. Any other suggestions about getting neighborhood preparedness coordinators that don't include asking Alete Keetch or eating ice cream?"

Everyone was silent for possibly the first time in this meeting. When Mayor Stone had wished him luck in pulling off a miracle without Alete's help, he hadn't realized just how much luck he would need.

ten

ALETE

Alete sat down at a picnic table in Snowdrift Springs Park and opened her laptop. She had spent the day working on the last of the details for Fall Market, helping out her parents with some Main Street Business Alliance issues, fielding some customer complaints at the inn, working with a business client who was arranging accommodations for his employees when they came for a corporate training at Team Up in the spring, making schedules for employees, lining up some maintenance and deep cleaning in different rooms and to the outside of the hotel, and managing her staff.

Even though it was the time of day she'd normally be leaving work, she still had advertisements for Colorado's tourism promotion to set up and supplies to order. And as warm as the day was and as beautiful as the park was when the leaves started changing colors, she just couldn't do it cooped up in her inn's office.

As she worked, she tried not to let her eyes wander to her phone so much. Her grandma was seeing her Parkinson's doctor today about getting the surgery that would hopefully allow her to be without her walker, and the doctor was supposed to text Alete the details about it. She knew how badly her grandma wanted this surgery, and knew that the sooner she could get it, the better.

Eyes on the laptop, she told herself. *You'll hear when the text comes in, and looking every two seconds won't get it here any quicker.*

There had been plenty of movement all around her from everyone else enjoying the warm day, but she'd only been working for thirty minutes when something caught her attention and she looked up. Zane was in the grassy field, throwing a Frisbee to his dog. She quickly moved to a spot on the table where a big tree was mostly blocking any view of her, so Zane wouldn't see her and come over to talk.

But she could still see him, and she kept finding herself looking up from her work to watch. His dog was cute. And each time the dog returned the Frisbee, Zane would crouch down and rub the sides of the dog's neck and say something to him.

It was clear that Zane loved his dog, and it was actually pretty adorable to see the two of them interact. His face was less intense and much more playful than it normally was. It was too bad he couldn't act around people as he did around his dog. Maybe he wouldn't be so bad then.

She kept trying to work, but she was spending more time watching Zane than creating ads. *Focus*, she told herself and looked back at her screen. It worked for a minute or two. Then she glanced up and saw that in the field to the side of Zane, where a bunch of teens were playing a pick-up game of flag football that seemed to be leaning more toward tackle football, one of the teens threw a ball as he was being tackled. The ball went way off course, and instead of its intended target, it flew hard and fast in Zane's direction.

A little girl was bent down tying her shoe by Zane with her back to the ball, and couldn't see that it was coming right at her. Alete leaped to her feet right as Zane noticed the ball. The ball was too close for him to turn to catch it, so he dove between the girl and the ball and the ball hit him square in the stomach instead of hitting the girl.

Then he went right from the dive into a tucking roll, and from the roll smoothly back to a standing position as if it was nothing. Then he picked up the football and tossed it in a tight spiral back to the group of boys who were watching him with their mouths dropped open. He gave them a salute with two fingers, and then picked up the Frisbee he'd been throwing to his dog. When he stood, his eyes fell on Alete, and she suddenly realized that she'd been watching with her mouth dropped open, too.

She closed her mouth and ducked back behind the tree like they hadn't just seen each other. Maybe he'd go away. She stayed still, not breathing, listening for sounds. For a moment, she thought she was in the clear, but then she heard leaves crunch under someone's feet, so she quickly looked around for an excuse as to what she had been doing hiding behind the tree instead of sitting at the table with her laptop.

"Hi," he said, as she was standing up after grabbing a stick out of desperation.

"Hi. I was just—" She held the stick up as if it would explain for her, but she realized that neither she nor the stick was going to be able to say anything remotely convincing as to why she'd been hiding, so she just set it on the table. "Working. I was working."

She sat back down in front of her laptop and clicked to bring up the screen that had gone dark. Luckily, it showed the ad images that she had been working on since she wouldn't have been able to say what she was working on last after the whole football, tuck-and-roll incident.

She could feel Zane behind her, probably wanting her to say more, but she remembered what had happened the last time they had tried to start over. Maybe if she just kept working, he'd go away.

But then his dog came over and nuzzled into her side,

so she reached down and let him smell her hand, then rubbed just behind his ears. He was a really cute dog, and it was obvious just by looking at him that he was well taken care of.

And for some reason, it made her think of how quickly he acted to save the girl from a football to the back. It made her wonder for the first time if maybe there was a part of him that did care about people. She had seen a part of him that she hadn't seen before, and it made her want to get to know him more. Not a lot more, but a teeny tiny bit more. Preferably at a time when he hadn't just caught her hiding behind a tree.

And it had nothing at all to do with the fact that he was actually wearing a t-shirt. He wasn't a big, bulky-muscled firefighter like she probably would've pictured before meeting him. He was lean, trim, and defined, and, okay, there may have been a little bit of stretching of his t-shirt across a couple of those muscles. That crooked smile he had given her probably would've been attractive if he hadn't been wearing it because he clearly knew she had been hiding behind that tree.

Impressively agile or not, adorable with his dog or not, fine-looking in a t-shirt or not, this was a man trying to destroy their town traditions.

The dog nuzzled into her even more, so she reached down with both hands, rubbing the sides of his neck. He was surprisingly soft. Not that she wanted a dog of her own, but for someone else's dog, he was okay. "It looks like you've got a pretty amazing dog."

"Second best dog in the world."

She raised an eyebrow and looked in Zane's direction. "*Second* best? I sense a story here. Who is the best?"

"Oliver. I had him when I was a kid. I'm pretty sure no dog will ever be able to take first place from him."

"He must've been a good dog. What was one thing you loved about him?"

"Just one?"

She nodded, and he looked up for a moment, thinking, showing off smooth cheeks that she wanted to reach out and lay her hand on. Surprised by the thought, she chided herself for even having it.

"He reminded me about everything important. It didn't matter how forgetful I was, he had my back and would remind me."

"Oh, that *is* helpful. I had my grandma's house for that."

His brows knit together. "Her house?"

She nodded. "She lived at the other end of the same block as us, and we had to walk past her house on our way to Nestled Hollow Elementary. I'm the youngest of four, so the year I was in first grade and my oldest brother was in fifth, he sprained his wrist. He kept taking off the wrist brace, and whenever my grandma saw him without it, she'd remind him to put it back on.

"In the mornings, he took it off to shower and get ready and usually forgot to put it back on. When we got to my grandma's house on our way to school, he'd remember and run back home to get it. He had that brace for six weeks, and by the time he stopped wearing it, my grandma's house was cemented in our brains as the object to make us stop and wonder if we forgot anything, then we'd run back home and get it."

"First grade, huh? So you walked past it through almost all of elementary school. Did it keep reminding you?"

She nodded. "Even as I walked past it to get to the middle school and the high school. It's still reminding me of things today."

"Does she still live there?" A smile was playing at the corners of his mouth. It was kind of cute. Maybe this guy wasn't so bad.

"Nope. She has Parkinson's and an inner ear issue, so she moved in with my parents a year ago. I bought her house. You know, to keep it in the family."

"Ahh, so you live there. Does this mean you never forget anything?"

"Like it's a superpower."

He looked at his dog for several long moments so she took the opportunity to look at Zane. He was a resident of Nestled Hollow. She loved the people of Nestled Hollow. Sure, some of them could be a little annoying or frustrating, but they largely got a pass because they were citizens of the town she loved, and, therefore, she loved them. She could extend the same courtesy to Zane. She *should* extend him the same courtesy.

She paused with a hand still on the dog's neck. Maybe she hadn't given Zane enough of a chance to start over when he'd tried to apologize to her in Elsmore's Market. She cleared her throat and turned on the bench so she was facing him. "What do you think about trying to start over again?" He quirked an eyebrow that she took as a yes. "Hi. I know we met under volatile circumstances, but—"

"I rather enjoyed our first meeting."

"Oh," she paused, "right. The hotel. I wasn't thinking about that."

"You forgot so quickly, even with the Grandma's House Superpower *and* even after I saved you from a lightbulb emergency."

She laughed and tried not to be embarrassed at that memory coupled with her very recent hiding-behind-the-tree memory. "I definitely haven't given you enough credit for that. Maybe we should go back to that and start fresh." She stood and held out her hand. "Hi, I'm Alete Keetch. It's nice to meet you."

He shook her hand. "Zane Collins. Nice to meet you, too." He gave a nod to her laptop on the table. "Do you always work in the park?"

"Only when it's this nice outside." She sat back down at the table and motioned to the bench, inviting him to sit. It was probably a bad idea to welcome him to stick around for longer, but she was impressed that things had been actually going well between them. It was surprising enough that she hadn't thought before extending the invitation.

He sat, but in the opposite direction— with his legs out instead of under the table, and leaned his back against it.

"I hate to talk shop on such a beautiful day," Zane said, "but in the interest of starting over, I would love to be able to understand where you're coming from a bit more."

She wasn't sure it was wise to move the conversation away from the dog and her grandma, but she gave him a slow, uncertain nod. It was enough that he continued.

"From what I can gather, you're not against Nestled Hollow getting prepared for a disaster, right?"

"Nope."

"Then help me to understand why you're fighting it so much."

She stared at her screen that had already darkened again, thinking. How could she get him to understand her side? She took a deep breath. "Have you ever heard the phrase, 'A single death is a tragedy; a million deaths is a statistic'?"

Zane nodded.

"I'm fighting it because you're only caring about the statistic, not the tragedy."

His expression changed quickly from confusion to disbelief to wariness. Finally, he said, "So what is it you're saying? That you would choose to only save one life when you could save a million? Or that you should save one person, even if it means sacrificing a million people? Or that we shouldn't care about the million people at all?"

She should've known that was what he would pull from it. She rolled her eyes. But part of her really liked that he stood up for what he believed in. He didn't just back down at the first sign of conflict.

"I'm saying that I care about the one. Every single one of the ones. That they aren't just a group— they're all different, unique, and have different needs. I'm saying people matter. As individuals. If you care about the one, *that's* what will save the millions."

Zane studied her for a few moments, his eyes narrowing, his jaw clenching and relaxing, clenching and relaxing. He might be trying to hide it, but he was getting more and more frustrated as this conversation continued. "And you think I don't care about people."

"When you don't care about what matters to them, and you don't care to see what's fueling them, it's hard to think that you do. You haven't cared to find out about the things you're proposing to cut. And as far as I can tell, you haven't even been talking to people to find out what they want. I mean, I've had three or four people come to me to ask if I knew why you wouldn't even respond to their invitations to come over for dessert. Is that how you show you care?"

Zane stood like he was irritated enough that he could no longer sit. And the way his voice came out tightly controlled, it was clear that he was, indeed, rather irritated. "Okay, then how about you continue on, saving your one person at a time, and I'll worry about saving the entire town."

But she had stopped listening before the end of his sentence because she happened to glance at the screen of her phone when it lit up with a text. Two parts caught her eye—the name of her grandma's Parkinson's doctor as the sender and the words "bad news."

Emotions slammed into her before even reading more. Emotions that she didn't want to experience right here in front of Zane. "I've got to go." She forced the emotions down, willing them not to come to the surface as she slapped her laptop shut, scooped it under her arm, and took off across the field, phone clutched tightly in her hand, breaths coming in ragged.

Lightheadedness made everything swirl. She didn't know if it was from breathing too fast or not breathing enough or a combination of the two— all she knew was that she needed to get somewhere safe, quickly.

Once she reached the other side of the field and went down the pathway leading to Snowdrift Springs, she opened the text and read it as she stumbled alongside the creek toward the bridge.

> Dr. Allen: I know you wanted to be updated about your grandmother's visit. I'm sorry to be the bearer of bad news. She told me that she is interested in DBS surgery. There are several reasons why she isn't a good candidate, but the main one is that she's not responding to the medication I've given her. DBS only works on patients who respond to it. I know this is news that neither of you wanted to hear, but there is nothing we can do to reduce your grandmother's symptoms.

No. This was going to crush her grandma. For Alete's entire life, the grandma she knew was active and full of life and joined in everything. She was independent and feisty and didn't let anything stop her. Getting the news that this thing that was stopping her was not only permanent but was something that was going to worsen with no way to stop it or lessen its effects was too much.

Many people in their eighties couldn't be very active. Her grandma just wasn't one of them. Alete had always figured the woman would be running circles around them all until the day she died. She might have a good day here and there, but for the most part, she was now going to be tied to that walker for the rest of her life.

At the thought of how this news must've hit her

grandma, Alete dropped to the bench by the bridge and sobbed. She sobbed for what her grandma was going to have to live without.

She sobbed knowing how much this news was going to crush Ammie.

She sobbed for her soccer teammate who was now permanently out of the game on injury.

And she sobbed for the grandma— and her best friend in the world— who wasn't going to be able to do all she wanted to.

eleven

ZANE

Zane watched in stunned disbelief as Alete hurried across the field. When she disappeared down a trail, he turned to Ranger. "What do you think, boy? Was that her way of telling me she hated what I said?"

His comment had come out frustrated and was plenty rude. But to just leave in the middle of a conversation? Their chat had started out pretty enjoyable, which had surprised him. She had gotten him thinking that she was a rational human and that they could actually talk through their disagreements. Maybe when she started talking about not saving the many so she could save the few, he should've guessed the conversation wouldn't end well.

Infuriating woman. He wanted to go back to Stockton and Mayor Stone and Amy and everyone else who thought he should work with Alete and tell them that he tried but it just wasn't going to happen.

No. He wasn't just going to walk away. If he was going to keep getting pushed in her direction by everyone around him, he was going to finish this conversation with her. He wasn't just going to walk away without doing everything he could. If she was going to keep spouting nonsense, well, *then* he could walk away with no guilt at all.

"Come on, boy," he said to Ranger, and he and the dog strode across the field. The more he walked, the more conversations played in his head of just what he wanted to say to her. The more perfect comebacks he came up with.

As soon as he and Ranger headed down the path to Snowdrift Springs, he looked across the lower field, trying to see which direction she'd gone. She'd had a bit of a head start, but he didn't think it had been enough for her to get past the fields.

Then, as he glanced at the path that ran alongside the creek, he spotted her sitting on a bench and he headed right for her, already biting back the insults forming on his tongue.

She didn't look up until he was within a couple of yards of her. When she did, he could see that she'd been crying. Enough that her eyes were red and tears were still on her face.

She batted at the tears as if she was angry that they were there. "What."

"I—" All the fight that had fueled his march across the fields and down here whooshed out of him, and he suddenly had to know what could've caused her to look so sad. Surely it hadn't been their conversation. She hadn't seemed close to tears at all. Their conversation at the combined Main Street Business Alliance and city council meeting had been much more heated, and that hadn't affected her like this.

"Is everything okay?" The words sounded stupid even to him. But still, he wanted to reach out and comfort her.

She looked down at the phone in her lap, turning it over and over. He took a chance and sat down on the other end of the bench, slightly angling her direction, hoping that his presence wasn't making her even more upset.

Finally, she heaved a big breath and said, "It's my grandma."

Zane hadn't realized exactly how much he had been hoping that he hadn't been the cause of her distress until those words let him know that he wasn't.

He stayed silent, in case she wanted to share more. After a few heartbeats that felt like minutes, she said, "She's been super active her whole life, and now she has a disease that won't let her be. But there's a surgery. We were so excited because it was supposed to help a lot, and —" She picked up her phone, like it was going to tell the rest of the story for her, then took a deep breath and said,

"—the doctor just texted to say that it won't. This is going to devastate her."

She let out a frustrated growl and wiped a new tear that had spilled out. "And me, apparently." She looked off in the other direction like she wasn't okay showing weakness like this.

"I'm sorry. That must be hard." Zane didn't know what to do or say. Part of him wanted to wrap his arms around her and protect her from all the pain she was feeling and tell her that it would all be okay. But he had been a jerk just moments before. And, to be honest, he was about to come down here and be a jerk again. That didn't really entitle him to any kind of comforting role.

So he just sat next to her and stared out across Snowdrift Springs and the lower field while she sniffed occasionally. Ranger knew what to do, though. He must've sensed her distress, so he got down on his stomach right next to her and lay his head on her feet.

After a good ten minutes of him wondering multiple times if it would be better if he left but stayed because she seemed to need someone near her, she took a long, slow breath, wiped away the last tear, and then turned toward him. "Thank you. I wouldn't have guessed how much I needed someone to just sit by me right now."

He didn't think he'd done enough to warrant a "You're welcome," so he gave a nod in acknowledgment. Maybe he should've given an apology for being a jerk, especially when she had something upsetting going on, but it felt like that would make this about him.

As soon as he made a move to get up, she briefly placed a hand on his knee. His eyes flew to her hand, then to her face as soon as she moved it. He knew the gesture was the universal sign to get him to pause just a moment, but even if he hadn't known that he wouldn't have moved. He seemed paralyzed by her touch, and he didn't quite know why.

"I'll help."

His eyebrows knit together in confusion.

"I know we don't agree on the methods, exactly, but I think your heart is in the right place, and I want to help."

He had not seen that coming.

His recent jerkiness aside, he wasn't actually one hundred percent convinced that he wanted her help. Things had mostly been going fine without her intervening, and he worried that if she stepped in to help, she'd constantly thwart his plans and they'd argue nonstop.

But there were some parts, like needing to find out which people to contact, where her advice could move things along more quickly. And it would keep the mayor— and everyone else—off his back about asking for her help. He would just keep her out of the other things.

He smiled. "I would love to have your help in making a list of people who might be good block captains to serve as neighborhood preparedness coordinators."

She smiled back. "You've got it. It would probably be easiest to come up with the list if we could look at the map in the city building. When are you free?"

"Whenever you and the room are."

Within about five seconds, Alete had Gloria on the phone and they were chatting like they were BFFs. Eventually, she asked when the conference room was free and looked at Zane. "Tomorrow at three work?" He nodded, and it wasn't long before she hung up the phone and said, "See you tomorrow, then."

As she gathered her laptop and phone and headed back up the path to the upper field, he just stared after her, thoughts of frustration and attraction battling it out in his head. He wasn't sure if agreeing to work with her was a great idea or the worst one ever.

———

Zane arrived in the conference room at ten to three. Alete arrived not long after him, but by the time she finished making small talk with Gloria at the front desk and Mayor Stone just outside his office, she was several minutes late.

She did look happier when she walked in than she was when he saw her yesterday. Taking her small-talk lead, especially after they'd connected the day before, he asked, "How's your grandma?"

"Um, about as depressed as you'd expect her to be. Now, tell me what you've got in mind."

So he explained that with a population the size of Nestled Hollow, he would like five or six block captains. People who would be responsible and willing and able to spend a good amount of time getting things set up over the next few months.

"See these lines here?" She ran her finger along a line that was only slightly wider than the lines dividing each property line.

He leaned in closer to see them and was suddenly aware of the fact that they had never been this close before. How had he not noticed that she smelled like spicy sweet vanilla when they were disagreeing at the meeting, or when he was sitting by her on the bench?

Or the way she ran a finger over her bottom lip when she was concentrating? It took him a moment to get his head back in the game and remember that he was looking for the lines.

"The city is already divided into seven neighborhoods. They're all named, and most people who live here know the name of their neighborhood, or at least they've heard them before. We don't use them tons, but if you're good with seven groups, it would be a convenient way to divide them for the block captains."

"Seven is great."

Alete studied the map, one neighborhood at a time.

For a couple of neighborhoods, she immediately gave him a name of an individual or a couple that she thought would be perfect. For others, she would put a finger on a home while she searched through the rest and would give him names after looking at them all.

"What do you think about—"

"Shush."

He should've known better than to interrupt when that finger was on her lip.

She gave the last name, and he looked down at his list. For all seven neighborhoods with their strange names, he had a first-choice and a second-choice block captain for each. And it had taken less than twenty minutes. It could've taken him weeks to get to this point on his own.

"Would you like me to ask them if they'll be block captains?"

He shook his head without looking up. "I'll do it." He had a list of things that they'd need to agree to do, and he wanted to make sure they were willing and weren't planning to back out later when they found out all it entailed.

Now he just needed her to leave. Because she smelled way too good and having her so near was making it hard for him to remember that she was the enemy. If he wasn't careful, she was going to worm her way into more of his plan, and that would spell disaster.

"How about planning the activities for the block

captains and the neighborhoods? I've got some ideas of some things that could really—"

"Thanks, but I've got it." He finally looked up from his list, and then held the clipboard up. "Thank you for this. It really helps." Then, even knowing she wanted to talk more about it and knowing that it was rude to accept the help and not be gracious about it, he turned and left the room first.

Yep, he was a jerk once again. A jerk who was developing way too many feelings for someone he had no business even thinking about.

twelve

ALETE

Alete made an unplanned stop by her parents' to see her grandma after she left All Nestled Inn on Wednesday, and found Ammie sitting at the kitchen table, staring at nothing. There wasn't even a book or magazine in front of her that she'd been reading. Her heart broke to see what this disease was doing to her normally happy and full-of-life grandma.

"Ammie, how long have you been sitting here?"

She shrugged.

Alete put her things down on the table and sat facing her. "I hate seeing you so sad."

"Well, between my balance problems and my shuffling walk both being permanent, there's not much I can do, so you better just get used to it."

Alete pulled her bag toward her. "George's niece came

to visit him and brought him enough peaches to share. Aren't they the most beautiful things you've ever seen? Come on. Help me peel and cut them up."

She stood and walked over to the sink in the island, but her grandma stayed where she was. Alete turned on the water to wash them off, and eventually, her grandma heaved a big sigh, pushed herself up with help from the table, and used her walker to go around the island and join her.

As they both peeled the peaches, her grandma's hands shaking slightly, Ammie said, "Tell me another story about the hot Fire Chief."

"I don't have another story to tell. I haven't seen him in a week." Alete had offered to help, and he let her— for twenty minutes. He hadn't asked for another thing since then. She wished she had known soon after the fire on the mountain how badly she wanted to help.

If she had, she could've gone to the mayor and city council and told them that she would be over emergency management and they could keep Chief Stockton as fire chief. She would gladly organize block captains and neighborhoods and plan activities for them to bond and get prepared and...Okay, she didn't actually know how to prepare a city for an emergency.

Once she did know what needed to happen, though, she knew how to pull it off in the best way.

"But you have thought about him, right?"

"Ammie, I can honestly say that I haven't thought about Zane for a few days."

At her grandma's lifted eyebrow, she amended. "Okay, a day."

The eyebrow stayed lifted, though. Ammie knew her too well. "A few hours. Okay, a few minutes. I don't know why I keep thinking about him so much! I mean, he's clearly a pain. But he's just got this passion and drive, and I like that he wants so badly to help.

"I mean, everything he does is *completely* wrong for Nestled Hollow and he's so arrogant and bull-headed that he can't stop thinking for two seconds that he already knows everything. He figures he did all of it in Springvale, so he must know how to do it in Nestled Hollow, even though they're nothing alike."

She took a deep breath. "But yeah. I think about him too much and I hate that I do. Stop laughing, Ammie."

"Not a chance," her grandma said, still chuckling. Then, after pretending to wipe a laugh tear away from her eye, Ammie said, "Okay, then, how about you re-tell me the story about the tight shirt and the dive-rolling to save the little girl and the athleticism? Or about him being un-showered and freshly heroic at the hospital. Both of those really cheered me up the last time you told them."

Alete laughed. "I see what you're trying to do, Ammie, and I'm not falling for your matchmaking. He's too rude and arrogant and..."

"And hot?"

"Ammie! Maybe I should be setting *you* up with him."

"You'd get no complaints from me there."

Their laughing and bantering brought back that spark in her grandma's eyes that she was used to seeing. But much too quickly, it disappeared again. No amount of cheering her up with stories was going to get her over being sad about her impaired mobility. She set down the knife and turned to face her grandma.

"You have several friends with walkers or wheelchairs or canes, right?"

Ammie nodded. "If you're trying to make me feel less alone in my problems, that's not going to work because that's not my issue."

"I'm not. Shush. Now list them off for me."

She leaned against the counter and looked up at the ceiling. "Let's see, there's Beth, Margie, William, Dorothy, Helen, Kenneth, Harold, Francis, and Carol. I think that's it."

"So, counting you, that's five with walkers, two in wheelchairs, and three with a cane, right?"

Her grandma nodded slowly. "Sounds right."

"That's ten people."

"So?"

"Ammie! That's enough to start a soccer team!"

Ammie dropped the knife to the counter and turned to face Alete, that spark returning to her eyes. "How?"

"I'll ask the pastor if we can meet in the social hall at the church. There are wooden floors there, so no problem for the wheels on the walkers or the wheelchairs. No tufts of grass to trip on. We can run it like I do our other team. We'll split into two groups by drawing sticks so it's always switching up."

"There are probably several who have never played."

"That's okay," Alete said. "I'll teach them. And then I can be the one on the sidelines blowing the whistle, refereeing, and smack-talking, and you can be the one playing."

Ammie reached out and put her hands, still sticky from peeling the peaches, on Alete's shoulders. "I'm going to be on a soccer team again?" Then, in a yell aimed at the ceiling— or possibly at the whole world— she said in as loud a voice as the Parkinson's would let her, "I'm going to be on a soccer team again!"

Alete didn't know how easy it was going to be to talk the other nine less-mobile residents of Nestled Hollow into being on the team, but if that was what was going to bring the spark to her grandma's eyes again, she would do everything she could to make it happen.

Her phone buzzed with a text, so she rinsed off her hands and picked it up. It was Zane, and the text read, *I could use some help with the block captains. Are you free?*

So the man *could* ask for help. She closed out of the text.

"You're not going to answer him?" She hadn't noticed that her grandma had leaned in close enough to read the text.

Alete set the timer on her phone for ninety minutes. "Not yet. I'm going to make him wait." As much as she wanted to jump at the chance to help, she didn't want to make him think that he could just use her whenever it was convenient and then block her out of everything when it wasn't.

Plus, she didn't want him to feel like he could control how she spent her time. It was one of the reasons why she'd gravitated toward a job where she was the boss because she didn't want a boss to be able to tell her what to do. If she was going to help, it was going to be on her own timetable.

———

Alete walked from the inn to the fire station at nine, right when she and Zane had agreed to meet. No one was in the open bay with the fire truck, so she headed to the office in the back corner and found him.

She had been in this office before, back when Stockton was the Chief. It looked so different now. Everywhere was neat and clean and organized and less cluttered than she'd ever seen it. Zane looked up from where he stood behind the desk, looking at some papers.

"What do you need my help with?" She hadn't realized that she had a thing for a guy in a uniform until she saw him standing there. He wasn't even wearing the full uniform, and it still got her. The button-down shirt was draped over the back of his chair, and he was wearing a t-shirt that said NHFD across the chest in big letters. She had to work to keep her eyes on his.

Eyes that just happened to be filled with passion and drive. Maybe it was safer to look at those lean muscles.

"I went to each of the block captains you recommended, and they all said yes, miraculously. I didn't even have to use your backup suggestion for any of the neighborhoods."

She smiled a little at having chosen her people well.

"I had them in here for a meeting a week ago and gave each the packet they needed with a link to the forms to fill out, and no one— not a single person— has gotten back to me or filled out the forms. And that was a week ago. I need to move forward in this area, but that's stopping me."

He reached up and rubbed the back of his neck. "Any ideas on how I can get them to respond?"

It was cute, seeing that brash confidence melt just barely enough to ask for help.

"What was in the packet you gave them?"

He handed her a manila envelope with papers inside. She pulled them out and started looking.

"That top form is a printout of the one I emailed. It asks for their own information— questions about who's in their household, their strengths and weaknesses, resources, background knowledge, and things like that, as well as a questionnaire about their willingness to learn more about different things.

"Right behind it— yep, that one— is a list of everyone in their particular neighborhood along with their addresses and phone numbers. The rest are the forms they need to fill out when they've gotten each resident's email address, so they can email the link to the form for them to fill out. They can either take a tablet with them to each neighbor and wait as they fill it out, or just get their email address, send it to them, then follow up later."

Alete flipped through the pages upon pages of forms. She had never seen so many forms in one place before. "Zane, no one likes filling out forms. Especially not this many."

She looked up in time to see the hurt look on his face before it quickly changed to resolve. "I do."

"No, Zane, all of this is daunting. Do you expect them to just go door to door to get this info? Did you give them anything to motivate them?"

"The motivation is being able to help the community be safe."

"You found the most boring way possible to do this. Organize neighborhood block parties. Then, when everyone comes together, the block captains can have tablets on a table with the form for each person to fill out."

"Block parties," he said, his tone flat. He shifted his weight and crossed his arms. "Are you telling me that your beloved town won't do anything unless it is fun?"

She dropped the packet back on his desk. "This isn't about fun. It's about looking out for each other, and that's exactly what the block captains are supposed to do, right? I mean what's going to happen in a big emergency that affects an entire neighborhood? Is the block captain supposed to check on every single person because he or she is the only person who knows everyone's details?"

"Yes!" He took a step toward the side of his desk, and she mirrored his move, so they were still facing each other, only the desk separating them. "That's exactly what they are signing up to do."

"That's a stupid way to set it up!" Heat built in her chest, spreading to her arms and legs, up her neck, and to her face. She could practically feel her heart beating in her neck, pumping that super-heated blood.

He took one more step to the side, and she again matched it, the desk no longer between them. "It's a proven method. I've seen it myself."

"Where? In Springvale? Just because something worked there doesn't mean it will here." He didn't understand where he was going wrong, and he was so very wrong.

He took a step closer to her. "How do you know if you won't give it a chance?"

She took a step closer, too, leaving less than a foot between them. "Because this is *my* town and I know them."

He took a small step closer, lessening the gap between them even more. His blood must've been super-heated, too, because she could feel the heat building up between them. "I've gone to school for this. I've spent hundreds of hours outside of school studying this. I've implemented an entire emergency preparedness plan in a city with over a hundred and seventy-thousand people. I've dedicated my life to helping people be safe since I was eight. What makes you think you're the bigger expert on what to do?"

She was trying to formulate a response, but there was that fire in his eyes as he argued about something that mattered enough to him to get this upset about it. And all the sticking up for what he believed in. And with that blasted t-shirt showing off those muscles he used for protecting people and the heat that had been building between him, all she could think about was his lips.

She kept trying to pull her eyes away from them and say something intelligent, but then she saw his eyes flick to her lips.

Maybe he closed the gap. Maybe she did. Maybe they

did at the same time. All she knew was that she suddenly had her lips on his, her arms around those strong shoulder muscles she'd been trying not to look at. His lips were warm against hers, his hands firm on her hips, and at least one of them had a heart beating loud enough to be heard.

All the heat both of them had built up through defending the things they cared about poured into the kiss. And maybe all the heat that had been building up between them since that night when he'd first come to town.

Then they both seemed to realize what they were doing at the same time and they both broke apart. She was sure that her face held the same look of shock that his did. They both moved to the spot they had been standing in when the conversation started, with the desk between them.

"I just kissed the enemy," she said, dazed. "You just kissed the enemy," she yelled. "What are we doing?"

Zane looked down at the papers on his desk while they both breathed in quick breaths.

"I...I don't know what happened," Zane said, unbelief in his voice.

Neither did she. Yet at the same time, it felt like it all had been building to this.

She put a hand on her forehead. "Well, I'm not just going to walk out of here right now, because then things would be super awkward the next time we meet. So here's how it's going down." She dropped her hand. "You're the expert on *what* to do. I won't argue with you on that one bit. I'm the expert on *how* to get this town to respond in the way you want them to. Don't argue with me on that one."

An amused smile played across his face and it was cute. So she kept going. "Most of this town knows each other, but we don't all know everyone. If you have your block captains go door to door, *they* will, of course, get to know each person. But everyone won't get to know everyone else."

He nodded, so she figured he might be listening. If nothing else, he wasn't arguing, which was pretty huge.

"Try to bring them all together in a meeting, and you won't get many to attend. Bring them together at a neighborhood party where they can socialize and talk to each other, then everyone will get those tighter bonds. They'll know about each other's needs and look out for each other. *Then* the block captains will get their forms in, and you'll be more successful."

Miracle of all miracles, Zane gave a nod and said, "Okay, I will."

"All right. Now I'm going to leave." She took two steps toward the door and then turned to look back at him. "And this—" she pointed back and forth between them, "—isn't going to be awkward next time we see each other. Got it?"

He flashed that amused smile again. She gave a frustrated growl as she left his office. He was too freaking adorable to be the enemy.

But he is the enemy, she reminded herself as she sunk against the wall outside his office, feeling like she'd just been swept up in a landslide and was no longer sure which direction was up. He was the enemy, and she'd just made things even more difficult than they already were.

thirteen

ZANE

By lunchtime, Zane was still stunned that he had kissed Alete. Alete! Yes, she was on his mind a lot. Pretty much constantly. But when he'd asked for her help, a kiss was the last thing he'd expected to happen.

Not that he hadn't thought of it happening in those first few moments of semi-awakeness in the mornings. But at that time of day, he'd also thought of having a fire hose connected to something like a jet pack filled with water. He was expecting the kiss to come true about as much as he was expecting to have the sudden ability to fly.

But now he couldn't stop thinking about the kiss that was just as fiery as the look he often saw in her eyes. Or how impressed he was that she wouldn't back down from a fight. Or the way he felt more alive when he was around her. As if her passion fueled his.

He and Ranger walked down the street to Joey's Pizza and Subs— a restaurant that he had grown to love since he moved here, especially since they had no problem with Ranger being inside on a leash. He walked in and what he had come to realize was the usual crowd, as well as a few people at tables who rotated in and out, all turned to see who had just walked in.

He gave a nod at the room in general and then walked up to the counter. He had ordered there enough times that when he stepped up to the line, Joey said, "The usual sandwich?" He nodded, paid, and took a spot at the table he always sat at if it was available— the one where he could see the entire room and the door with no one at his back.

After a few minutes of waiting, Stockton walked in with his wife and when the room turned to see who walked in, *all* of them reacted. Lots of "Hey, how you doin'?" "Good to see you!" "Hiya, Chief" and handshakes.

When Stockton and his wife turned to walk up to the counter, he noticed Zane, and the two of them walked over. Stockton shook his hand, re-introduced his wife, although they had already met at the retirement party, and said, "Do you mind if we join you?" He told them they could, and they went up to the counter to order.

Back in Springvale, he'd sought out the kind of anonymity he just experienced when he walked into the room, where people generally ignored you whether they knew you or not. But for the first time that he could recall, he didn't like that he felt like he was on the outside in the town where he lived.

———

There were so many different aspects to preparing a town for a major disaster. When Zane had first stepped into this position, he'd felt the weight of all of them at once. He had made lists of everything and prioritized them, and now everything felt like it was falling into place.

He had set up a meeting with the local pastor to see what help he could get from the church in a disaster, and from what he'd heard from his crew, Pastor Iver was a pretty easygoing guy when it came to stuff like this. Good. Maybe he could be in and out of this meeting quickly, and on to tackling the next thing on his list.

He had just parked his truck in the parking lot of the church and was about to get out when he saw Alete walking into the building with a group of disabled elderly men and women. What was she doing here with them in the middle of the week? Was this some kind of secret meeting? Was this how she managed to get everyone to do what she asked? By having these meetings with them?

Curiosity burned in him as he exited the truck and made his way toward the other end of the church where Pastor Iver had asked Zane to meet him.

Just like his crew had said, the gray-haired pastor was great to work with. He told Zane that he could "count on them for anything in a disaster" and to put the church on his emergency preparedness plans however he saw helpful.

He wished every step on his list of things to do was as easy as this one. With every pause in the conversation, though, Zane's mind went back to Alete and came up with new scenarios of what she might be doing.

"I haven't seen you at Sunday meetings yet," Pastor Iver said. "So before you go, would you like a tour of the church? I imagine it'd be easier to know how to use us as a resource if you've seen the place."

Zane hoped he hadn't looked too eager to take him up on his offer. The guy was practically offering to let him peek in on Alete's secret meeting. Pastor Iver showed him the other couple of offices in the back, then the chapel, then the meeting rooms for the youth and other groups, but Zane hadn't seen any signs of Alete.

All along the side of the building they were at now, though, he kept hearing banging sounds and muffled yelling and couldn't guess what could possibly be going on. The pastor didn't seem concerned, though, and showed him a storage area where they had a bunch of blankets, a good number of flashlights, cases of water, and other emergency equipment. "I can get you a list of everything we have here for emergencies if you'd like."

Then he led him out of the storage area and down the

hall, stopping at a door. "This room might be the most helpful if we have to house a group of people after they've been evacuated. It's a little occupied at the moment, so you might have to watch for a ball coming at your head, but we can peek in."

He opened the door and the two of them slipped into the room. It took a moment before Zane could make sense of what he was seeing. All of the elderly people he had seen entering the church were in this room, moving all around in their wheelchairs and with their walkers and canes, playing what appeared to be soccer. The ball was soccer sized but made of soft foam.

And Alete was on the sideline at center court, standing on a folding chair, her back to the wall, a whistle in her hand, watching the action. He and the pastor were in the corner and out of her line of vision. He just watched her watch the game, one hundred percent of her focus on the players.

He noticed that half of the players were wearing green pinny jerseys, and half were wearing purple. Some of them clearly hadn't been playing long, and some had probably spent a good amount of time on the soccer field in their younger years.

Even though the game and the players were slower moving than at other soccer games he'd seen, all were more fierce players than he ever would've guessed. Was this something elderly people commonly did in their free time? Or was this unique to Nestled Hollow?

He looked at Alete, who was calling out a combination of encouragement, smack talk, and refereeing to the players. He shook his head. Knowing what he knew about Alete, it was probably all her doing.

"Have they been playing here long?" he asked the pastor quietly. Although, with as much noise as was in the room and with a good portion of its occupants likely hard of hearing, he probably hadn't needed to be quiet.

Pastor Iver shook his head. "This is only their second time. The first time wasn't a game, though. Alete was just teaching them how to play since a handful of them didn't know. Isn't it quite a sight to see? Only Alete could pull something like this off. Her grandma is that one over there with the walker— the one that just pounded the ball to the other end. She's eighty-five and was playing with Alete's team on the field at Snowdrift Springs Park until just a month or two ago if you can believe that."

Zane's mind immediately went to that moment in the park when he'd seen her by the creek, crying after getting news about her grandma's illness. "How did this get started?"

The pastor shrugged. "Ammie wanted to play, but couldn't play on grass anymore. Soccer isn't really something you can play without a team, and Alete somehow convinced this lot to play."

"I'm learning that when she gets an idea in her head, there's not a whole lot that can stop her."

The pastor chuckled softly beside him. "You've got that right."

It took him a few moments of watching the chaos of wheelchairs and walkers and canes and elderly before he could see any organization to it. The goals seemed to be an area marked by masking tape on the floor, and each side had someone in a wheelchair acting as a goalie.

"Nice kick, Beth!" both Alete and her grandma called out, and Beth held a wrinkled fist in the air in triumph.

"Oh, yeah?" a man with a walker said. "Well, check out this!" He missed his first kick, so then he used the other leg and kicked it out toward the crowd of players.

"I've got it!" A woman hit the ball with her cane, sending it rolling off to the side.

"Penalty," Alete's grandma called out. "Hands."

"It wasn't a hand, it was my cane!"

"Which is attached to your hand."

Zane chuckled. He was beginning to see a little bit of where Alete got her fighting spirit from.

"Alete! Tell her it counts!"

"I'm with Margie on this one," Alete said. "It's a third foot."

The woman, Margie, grinned.

Alete's grandma lifted her walker off the ground an

inch or two. "Hear that, players? That means those of us with walkers have six feet!"

And then Zane watched as the elderly players tried moving their walkers around to hit the ball instead of using their feet. Honestly, he couldn't tell if it was more effective or not.

As he watched them play, and Alete call out comments as if she knew every single person on the team well enough to know who to encourage and who to smack talk to, he let himself marvel at her for a moment. It was fun to see her in action when that action wasn't directed at messing with his plans.

And, he'd admit, thoughts of the kiss they'd shared crossed his mind more than once. It hadn't stopped crossing his mind for a while now. Mistake or not, it had been rather unforgettable.

His eyes were on Alete when he heard her grandma yell out, "Alete, we got our cheering section after all! Look — it's the hot fire chief!"

Zane might've been a little embarrassed if it hadn't been for the blush showing on Alete's cheeks as her head whipped in his direction and her eyes met his. Seeing her embarrassment at her grandma calling him the "hot fire chief" was so much better.

"Time!" Alete's grandma called from the middle of the court, letting go of her walker long enough to make the "T" sign with her hands. Then she shuffled her way with her walker to the side of the court where Alete was stepping down from her chair and nodded in Zane's direction.

Alete rolled her eyes at her grandma, but in a way that somehow didn't seem rude. More like playful banter between the two.

When the two of them neared him, Alete cocked her head ever so slightly to the side, and said, "Zane. I didn't expect to see you here."

"I can say the same about you."

"He came to talk to me about the church's role in an emergency," Pastor Iver said. "I offered to give him a tour."

Alete brushed some loose hair back in the direction of her ponytail. "That's great." She cleared her throat, and then looked down at her shoe as she rubbed it against a strip of hardwood.

"Yeah." Zane shifted his weight and put his hands in his pockets. "It's been helpful."

Alete's grandma let go of her walker and threw her hands into the air. "I thought you two had decided to *not* act awkward around each other after your kiss!"

Alete's cheeks reddened noticeably, and with the heat he felt in his own, he wouldn't be surprised if he looked just as flushed.

"Ammie!"

"You two..." the pastor motioned between Zane and Alete, "are together?"

"No!" they both said, a bit too forcefully.

"The kiss was just an accident," Alete said.

"You *accidentally* kissed?" the pastor asked, clearly confused. Or possibly he was being judgmental and was a really good actor.

Zane nodded. "A product of circumstances that we'll be sure to stay away from in the future."

Alete's grandma elbowed her and stage-whispered, "Introduce me."

"Oh, sorry. Ammie, this is Fire Chief Zane Collins. Zane, this is my grandmother, Annie Erickson."

Her grandmother held out her wrinkled hand and gave him a shake that was much firmer than he'd expected. "Call me Ammie. Ever since her oldest brother was a toddler and shortened 'Grandma Annie' to Ammie, that's what everyone calls me."

Ammie took a shuffling step back as if to see him more fully, appraising him. "I have to say, you're everything I expected and more. And I can't say I'd complain if you wanted to demonstrate that block and roll into standing and throwing a football move when you were protecting that little girl from a ball to the back. It sounded impressive."

"Ammie!"

"What? I'm an athlete. I appreciate athleticism."

Zane tried to hide his smile, but he couldn't manage

to. So Alete was not only noticing him, but she was telling her grandma about him.

"We clearly have to get back to the game now." Alete nudged her grandma to turn and head in the direction of the others.

"It was nice to meet you, Zane!" Ammie called out.

He stayed for a few moments, watching as Alete stepped back up on her chair and all the players looked at her, waiting for direction like they'd walk into battle next to her if she asked them to.

Maybe she was right. Maybe joining a bit in this community might make things easier.

After he thanked the pastor and said goodbye, he walked to the parking lot and pulled out his phone. He scrolled through his messages until he came to the first one from a Nestled Hollow resident asking him over for ice cream and accepted the invitation.

ALETE

As Alete walked from group to group, chatting with all her neighbors as she made her way to the food, she once again was blown away by the fact that Zane was able to set up block parties for all seven neighborhoods on the same night.

Several long tables were lined up, one after another, right in the middle of one of the streets in the center of her neighborhood, all filled with dishes each of the neighbors had brought. Two families had wheeled their barbeques to the middle of the street, too, and were grilling hot dogs and hamburgers.

And of course, there was a table with tablets, each with the link to the form Zane needed to be filled out so that if there ever was an emergency and they needed to be evacuated, they'd know who needed the most help, who had the most help to give, and whether or not everyone was accounted for.

By the time it started getting dark outside, Alete had eaten dinner, joined in a flag football game in the Klein's and Banks's front yards, sat and chatted with every single neighbor in her neighborhood, and filled out the form for her household of one. She was helping Sam set up some outdoor lights so they could keep socializing when she turned and bumped into Zane.

He looked as surprised to see her as she was to see him. He quickly glanced around, and then said, "I didn't know this was your neighborhood."

She motioned with her arm to all the people gathered. "In all its beauty. What are you doing here?"

"I've been checking in at all the parties."

"And?"

He stood tall and looked out over the group of people socializing and hesitated. Finally, he turned back to her. "They've been successful."

Alete crossed her arms.

"Okay, very successful."

"And have the forms been getting filled out?"

"This is the fifth party I've checked in on, and we are averaging about ninety percent so far."

Alete grinned. "I believe there are some words you feel compelled to say right now. I think Bill over there has a megaphone if you'd like to use it."

He shook his head. "I'm not about to say 'You were right' into a megaphone."

"Then say it just to me. And then I'll say to you 'I'm impressed that you pulled off seven block parties on the same night. That's some amazing work.'" She didn't miss the way his smile curved up just a bit and his chest puffed out just a little. "And then tell me what is next on the docket."

Zane sucked in a breath, and even looked over his shoulder at the street he must've parked on.

"You don't want to tell me!"

"It's not that. It's just..." He drummed his fingers on his leg. "Okay, fine. Maybe you'll have some ideas on how to run this. Do you know what a Go Bag is?"

She shook her head no. But she couldn't just stand there as they talked, looking at him in the glow of the street lights, without thinking about that kiss they'd shared. Or how she wanted to kiss him again. Or the way he looked when he was talking about his concern for the town. Or how those strong shoulders made him look like he could protect anyone. So she picked up an abandoned basketball at the end of the Carters' driveway and passed it to him.

He glanced at the basketball hoop at the side of their driveway, then back to her as she walked to it. He gave her a slight nod, then dribbled the ball as he made his way toward her. "If there's ever an emergency where you need to get out quickly, it's vital to have a Go Bag for each member of the household."

He maneuvered around her block and shot the ball, making a basket. Alete grabbed the ball as it came through the hoop and started dribbling it.

"The bag needs to contain paper copies of important documents and phone numbers, and all the things you might need for a good seventy-two hours. Now, some of the stuff is specific to each individual, and families will have to gather that on their own. Things like medications, documents, and clothing. But there are a lot of things that need to go in each person's bag that they might not have that could take a while to gather."

"And each person needs one?"

He was trying to block her from being able to turn around and shoot, and she was trying not to let the feeling of his shoulder and arms bumping into hers distract her. Even though his touch was *really* distracting her. So much for her plan to keep from thinking about that kiss.

"Every single person. If you get separated from the rest of your family, it's important you still have what you need."

She finally got her head back in the game and cut back, surprising him, and got free enough to make her own basket.

"Nice one." He grabbed the ball and dribbled it around her, attempted to make a shot, and missed, yet still got the rebound. "So I was thinking. Shopping for all the supplies you need for something that *could* happen, but might not, is something that's easy to procrastinate. And I don't want everyone to not be prepared if something goes wrong just because shopping for it never made it to the top of their to-do list."

She was the one doing the blocking this time, and with his extra height, she had to stay vigilant, pressing against his side so he couldn't easily make a shot while trying not to think about how it felt to have so much of herself pressed against him.

"So I was thinking I could bulk order the things on the list that every person needs, and then people can purchase the kits. That way they'll have them in their homes and will be more likely to gather their personal things and add that to their bags."

Alete paused just a moment to think how to answer, and he used the slip to make a basket. She got the ball back and dribbled it a few times, then grabbed it with both hands and just held it.

"When the fire started on the mountain last year, it was scary. It started not far from homes, and it spread alarmingly fast. For a while, the wind wasn't in our favor, and it was spreading toward houses. The sun was just setting, and the flames were visible from anywhere in the city. The heat of the fire...I was surprised how far out you could feel it."

He flinched. It was a small motion, but she still caught

it from the corner of her eye. He'd spent years fighting fires— he could probably picture every bit of it as real as if he'd been there.

"Our fire department responded within minutes, and within twenty-two minutes, we got help from Mountain Springs. From Silver Stone not long after that."

She started dribbling the ball again. "You saw what our town's emergency plan was like when you first came here. Tell me what you think happened at that point."

He tried blocking her, matching her footwork, keeping himself between her and the basket, but he was more distracted this time, more thoughtful. "My guess? People drove up to see the fire out of curiosity, blocking the firefighters from getting where they needed to go. When it was clear that homes were threatened, panic. Chaos. People scrambling into their homes, packing up everything they could fit in their cars, and trying to get away.

"Others were unwilling to leave when evacuated because they felt they needed to stay and defend their homes from looting. Definitely traffic congestion. And I'm sure there were people who didn't leave town because they had nowhere to go. Your inn and the other hotel were likely flooded with more people than they could take in."

She maneuvered around his defenses and made a shot. A beautiful shot, if she did say so herself. "That's a good guess. But no."

Zane had grabbed the basketball, but he just stood with it resting at his side between his hip and his wrist.

"The fire *did* bring spectators, but most walked, biked, or brought four-wheelers or side-by-sides, so they didn't block the firefighters. When it was clear that homes were in danger, everyone who had gotten close out of curiosity went home to home, making sure everyone made it out, helping them to pack up things they would need, and offering to help transport things.

"We didn't have an evacuation plan or a good plan of what to do with the evacuees, but we came up with one quickly. People showed up on Main Street with water bottles, blankets, and offers for people to stay in their homes. Twenty-seven families were evacuated, and within an hour, all twenty-seven families had a warm, comfortable place to stay, and all the restaurants banded together to make sure they had warm food."

"Wow. That's...impressive."

She grabbed the ball away from him and attempted a basket but missed the shot. He grabbed the rebound, this time dribbling the ball instead of just holding it.

"This town attracts good people, but that's only a small part of it. We aren't perfect, but we do look out for each other. The thing that made the difference is our town celebrations."

"Alete." He dribbled the ball and she blocked him, bumping into him as much as she needed to in order to keep him from scoring. "I know you love them, but right now, we need the money—"

She reached out and managed to steal his dribble and block him from taking it back. "And I think you're wrong to look there for the money, and I will very happily argue my point at some other time."

She flashed him a smile. Partly to annoy him, and partly because she really would enjoy that conversation.

"But what I'm saying is that we plan a lot of things in this town, and we do everything we can to get as many people participating as possible. That's what makes us close ranks and protect those in danger. Just giving people a sign-up sheet or an order form and letting them come in at their convenience to pick up their kits isn't going to foster community, a sense of belonging."

She took a shot and missed, but he grabbed it out of the air, holding it with both hands in front of him, stance wide. He took in a deep breath and blew it out slowly. Then he shook his head. "You're going to suggest something ridiculous, aren't you?"

She flashed him her brightest smile and knocked the ball out of his hands. "You better believe it."

He ran a hand through his hair. "Okay, fine. Give it to me."

"We make sure that the businesses in town carry everything that needs to go in the kits," she said, dribbling. "If it's difficult stuff to get, you can buy it in bulk if you'd like and still do your sign-up sheets. But spread the stuff throughout the businesses in town. Then have a big event where families come and go on a scavenger hunt to find everything we all need. Then we bring it all back to the high school gym, and we do a relay race where everyone packs up their bags."

He stepped up his blocking game and even reached to take away her dribble a couple of times. "This is not really your suggestion, right? You're just messing with me by suggesting the most complicated way to do an already large job?"

"I'll defer to your expertise on what to put in the bag," she said, bumping her backside into his side, trying to keep him away from the ball but very much feeling the zing of electricity rush through her at their touch. "Defer to mine on how to get the biggest percentage of the population to actually get it in their bags." She spun around and made a basket.

Neither of them grabbed the ball as it bounced into the grass. Zane studied her for a long moment, probably trying to decide if she was being serious and if he trusted her judgment. And looking at her in a way that she couldn't quite interpret but still sent heat up her spine.

Finally, he gave a quick nod and said, "Okay, I'll defer. Against my better judgment."

"Look at us." She grinned. "We disagreed, but came to an agreement without arguing."

"I've never been more proud." His voice came out sarcastic, but she could see a smile on his face in the light of the lamps.

It was times like these when Alete could actually imagine having a serious relationship. Maybe even marriage. She always figured she was much too headstrong to ever get along with someone, but look at them now. They didn't agree on a lot, but they were still being respectful and civil and all that. It was almost as if they were getting along.

ZANE

The town activity in the high school gym was ten minutes from starting when Zane's phone buzzed. He pulled it from its clip at his waist and saw his brother's name. He took a deep breath to mentally prepare himself for the call and then stepped into the hallway to answer.

"Hello, Wyatt."

"Hey, Zane. How are you?"

"I'm good. About to start a meeting with the entire town, so if this can be quick..."

"No problem. I was just calling to say hi and to give you the head's up that I told Mom and Dad that you moved since you never got around to it."

"Thanks." Honestly, he hadn't thought about calling to tell his parents about the move very often, but when he did, he had been feeling guilty about not having done it yet. So his "thanks" was a genuine one.

"And I told them that you're now the Fire Chief and Emergency Management Director. How's that going, by the way?"

"Moving right along. Hopefully, we'll get this town prepared before any snow falls."

"Good."

There was a pause for a long enough moment that Zane almost told his brother he needed to go, but then Wyatt said, "Mom and Dad said they're really proud of you and your new job title."

"Can we not do this?"

"What? I just said they're proud of you. I thought you'd like to know because I know how much that mattered to you."

"It's been a long time since it last mattered. I quit trying to get them to pay attention by excelling at things a long time ago, and my life is more peaceful for it. Don't try to drag me back in."

"You've always been smart for a little bro. I wish I had followed your lead and done something with my life, instead of vying for their attention in less... positive ways." There was a good long pause before he added, "Maybe someday I'll follow your lead and figure out how to quit caring about getting to get their attention, too."

That was the most real thing his brother had said to

him for as long as he could remember, and he was stunned into speechlessness. Finally, he managed to say, "I'm sorry, Wyatt. Call me anytime, okay? No sense in us continuing to go through it all alone."

"Will do."

Zane clipped his phone back into its holder and made his way back into the gym. For years— since Wyatt was about thirteen— Zane had seen him as just another person in his family who didn't care about him as much as they cared about going out and doing whatever they wanted to do. It hadn't ever occurred to him that his brother might have been going through the same things he was.

And that maybe Wyatt's reasons for making so many bad choices were the same as Zane's drive to excel. So much of his childhood was replaying in his mind, and he struggled to get his head back into the high school gym.

Alete walked to where he stood next to the small portable stage that had been set up at the north end and said, "You okay?"

Seeing her helped him to clear his mind and refocus on the event he was about to start. The room full of hundreds of families re-grounded him, too. He nodded. "Thanks for coming to help with this."

"Of course."

He glanced at the clock and saw that it was exactly seven. Time to start. He climbed the three stairs and stepped up to the microphone. Alete followed right behind him. He had asked her to join him on the stage because he had seen how much the town followed her. If they knew that she was on board with all of this, hopefully, they would be, too.

The room was filled with people, almost to capacity. He still couldn't believe that so many people would show up to something like this.

He had decided that this must be a town full of optimists, so it was important for him to let them know of the dangers that faced them. There was probably a good percentage of them who had lived in Nestled Hollow for long enough to have seen many of the dangers themselves, but he figured he should say it anyway for the benefit of the newer residents.

After he thanked them all for coming, he said, "I'm glad that so many of you came today, because having a Go Bag is important for everyone everywhere. It's especially important for us here, because Nestled Hollow has so many threats." He was so proud of himself for how easily the "us" came to him. He hadn't even thought about it before he said it.

"With that fire damage on the mountain, avalanches will be more likely, and when all the snow melts in the spring, it makes a landslide of mud not only possible but very likely. Raise your hand if you've ever seen some great snow for the ski season, then a few warm days hit somewhere about March, and Snowdrift Springs turned into a raging river overflowing its banks?"

A lot of people in the crowd raised their hands, and the people around them who didn't have their hands raised had worried faces. Good. It was like social proof that what he was talking about was real.

"An avalanche upstream can easily bring some pretty big debris down that river, too, causing a lot of damage. You've got a mountain on the other side of I-70. If there's an avalanche there, it could easily block any help outside of Nestled Hollow from even getting here."

He definitely had their attention now.

"I don't tell you this to scare you. Tonight is all about empowering you. If you have a Go Bag for every person in your family, you'll be so much safer no matter what happens. So what do you say we get them together?"

The crowd all shouted back "Yeah!" and other, more guttural cheers. This was actually fun. It was almost like he was leading a pep rally. He accomplished a lot when he was in Springvale, but he'd never had a crowd react to creating something like Go Bags with so much enthusiasm.

"You'll all get a list of the things that need to go in your bags, and you'll see that some of the things you'll have to add at home. Once you get everything in there on the list, if there's ever an emergency, will you have everything you need in that bag?"

Everyone shouted, "Yes!"

So he said loudly into the microphone, "No!" and everyone looked up with confused faces. He stepped aside and motioned for Alete to take the mic.

"There is one important thing that isn't going to fit in your backpacks, and that's bedding. If there's an emergency and you have to evacuate quickly, grab a sleeping bag if you can. Maybe even a small pillow. Chief Collins has made sure that there are some blankets in each of the evacuation sites, but there won't be enough to keep everyone comfortable. And one of the hardest things you might have to deal with is the effects of sleep deprivation because it impairs your ability to act in an emergency. Now, are you all ready to get those Go Bags filled?"

They all shouted "Yes" again, but this time, they seemed a little wary, like they were no longer sure there wasn't something else they hadn't thought of.

Alete handed the microphone back to him. "See these signs taped along the walls? Find the one with your neighborhood's name and your block captain's name. I've got a firefighter or EMT assigned to each neighborhood to help you, too. They'll give you instructions, and—" A kid's hand shot into the air. Zane hadn't asked for questions, but the ten- or eleven-year-old looked insistent, so he called on him. "Did you have a question before we get started?"

"Yeah. What do we get if all of us get our Go Bags ready?"

"What do you get?" He didn't even understand what the kid was asking.

"You know, like as a prize."

"You get to have what you need in an emergency."

"No, not that kind of prize! At school, when we all got our fire drill papers in, Principal Ploeger wore pajamas to school and shaved his head. And so did the firefighters and EMTs. What are you going to do if we all get our Go Bags ready?"

All the kids in the audience started chatting to the people around them about how cool that was. The worst part was that several adults were nodding their heads, too.

He had opened his mouth to say words that hadn't come to him yet when Joey shouted out, "I've got it!" He wished he had thought of something to say more quickly — he wasn't a fan of anything Joey shouted out. "You were talking about sleep deprivation and how it impairs you. If we get all our Go Bags completed, how about showing us firsthand what that can do? You two could go a night without sleep and document it for us."

"Ha, ha. No." He tried not to roll his eyes at Joey's suggestion. The man probably wanted the sleep deprivation to make him and Alete argue on camera. He seemed to enjoy the show when they had disagreed at the Main Street Business Alliance meeting.

But everyone else in the gym jumped on the suggestion, and he could see the excitement building in the room. He looked at Alete to see how she was responding. She shrugged and said, "Why not? It's for a good cause. Might be fun."

They stared at each other for a long moment, as thoughts of how that could possibly turn out ran through his mind. A part of him pushed away from the idea, worried about how much arguing could happen. And a part— possibly a bigger part, he admitted to himself— was drawn to the idea of spending hours with Alete.

Then he looked back at the crowd and thought about how different Stockton's reception at Joey's Pizza and Subs had been from his. He might only plan on this being his town for a short while, but he wanted that kind of connection with them more than he was willing to admit. And this was the kind of thing to get him there.

"Okay," he said into the microphone. "We'll accept that deal. If we get ninety percent of all residents with complete Go Bags, then Alete and I will both stay up for a full twenty-four hours, right here in the school. We'll post videos of how the sleeplessness is affecting us on the Nestled Hollow social media page. But you'll have a lot of work to do to make sure that everyone who isn't here tonight has their bags ready, too. Deal?"

It was a big ask. But having everyone working to make sure they all had Go Bags instead of taking on that monumental task himself would likely prove so much more successful.

The entire crowd shouted, "Deal!" This was surreal. He didn't even know towns that responded like this actually existed outside of Hallmark Christmas movies. He shook his head. If it got all of them to be personally prepared for a disaster, he would've been willing to do a lot more than simply stay up all night long.

Once they got the crowd separated into groups and headed off to do the scavenger hunt portion of the event before coming back to do the relay race to pack the bags, he and Alete were the only two left in the room.

"I'm impressed," Alete said as she walked toward him from where she'd been helping on the other side of the gym.

She had given him another genuine compliment. He didn't think that would ever get old. "You didn't think I would agree to it?"

"Well, I knew there was a little bit better chance at you saying yes since I wasn't the one asking."

"Ahh, but it's worse because we'll actually have to spend a good twelve of those twenty-four hours together." Although there was a part of him that really wanted to spend those twelve hours with her. As long as they could stay away from talking about how he should do his job.

"Ugh. *Twelve hours*. We could drive each other clinically insane in that amount of time."

"It's definitely a risk. What do you think the chances are that ninety percent will get their Go Bags ready?"

"When we were splitting everyone into groups," Alete said, "I found Whitney. She's going to put it in the paper and really sell it."

"So you're saying we might have to actually do this?"

She shrugged. "Unless you want us to not get our own Go Bags ready. Be holdouts. Encourage a few others to join us." The teasing gleam in her eyes really brought out the blue. Did he detect a note of flirting in there, too?

"I'm pretty sure they'd just make one for us."

With a mock-serious look on her face, she sighed and said, "I guess we just need to get resigned to our fate."

sixteen

ALETE

Alete sat in her office at the hotel, working through her monthly profit and loss reports, revenue and guest satisfaction targets, evaluation of advertising effectiveness, addressing which things most needed to go on the monthly budgets, and deciding how much of the flexible income should go to which items.

It was a job that took intense concentration for a good five hours if she wasn't interrupted. She had hotel manager friends she met at conferences that she kept in touch with who took several hours a day over a two-week time period to accomplish the same thing.

She was convinced that the reason why she was able to do so much and not have managing the hotel be her entire life was because she didn't let people distract her while she was doing it— or any of her other deep concentration tasks— so they didn't consume all day of every day.

She liked having an open door to her office, so her employees knew they could come to her for anything. But they also knew that if her door was shut, they had to stay away unless it was hailing scorpions, if the water in Snowdrift Springs suddenly changed to Dr. Pepper and was overflowing its banks, or if something else of biblical proportions happened.

It was especially important that they stay away for Five-Hour Day.

She was just getting into figuring out the total they had spent on cleaning supplies, laundry supplies, and disposables for the rooms when there was a timid knock at the door.

"Yes?" She tried to make her voice not sound as perturbed as she felt.

The door opened a crack, and Nikki poked her head in. "So sorry to bother you, but one of the guests is complaining of a bad sound coming from the ceiling fan in their room."

Once she dealt with the issue and reminded Nikki that she had empowered her to deal with those kinds of guest issues on her own, she tried to get back into what she had been working on.

To really concentrate and make progress, it felt like

she had to do the long hard task of climbing a giant rope ladder up to a platform high in the sky where she could work with a clear mind and focus on that one thing with intensity. Whenever someone came in and disrupted that concentration, it was like they threw a lasso up, caught her around the waist, and yanked her to the ground. Then she'd have to start the process over again.

Thirty minutes later, she got another knock on her door. She hadn't even answered before George poked his head in the door. "Hey, Boss. Just wanted to let you know that I checked on that ceiling fan noise, and it's an electrical problem. They won't be able to use lights in the room until I fix it, so Nikki's moving them to a different room."

She didn't respond immediately, assuming he was getting to the question he came in here to ask, but there didn't seem to be one. George realized it quickly, though, and said, "I probably should've just emailed you about it instead. Sorry for bothering you, Boss. I'll leave you alone now." He pulled the door shut.

Being pulled out of her concentration was so aggravating when she was working on something so intense that she couldn't even focus on restarting. Especially because every time she was interrupted, her mind went to Zane before she could stop it, so she had to banish thoughts of him before climbing the ladder again.

She stood and paced around her office for a moment before deciding that she needed a change of scenery. After gathering her papers and packing up her laptop, she announced to her staff that she was going to be working from home for the rest of the day and to call Ammie if they had any problems they couldn't solve.

When she got to her car, she sent her grandma a quick text.

> Alete: I'm working from home in Do Not Disturb mode. Do you mind fielding questions? She didn't need to explain further— her grandma knew the drill.

Ammie's response came quickly.

> Ammie: Don't you worry. I'll field them like a pro and only text you if flaming locusts attack the inn or animals start talking in complete sentences.

Ammie was the only person that Alete had on emergency bypass on her phone because she knew her grandma wouldn't text while she was in Do Not Disturb mode with anything short of someone's life being in danger.

As she drove home, her ex-boyfriend, Austin, popped into her mind. They had dated for quite a while back when she was new at running the hotel. She hadn't gotten so many things in place and running smoothly yet and it took a lot more of her time. A lot more Do Not Disturb time.

Even though she had given up thoughts of marriage after Josh, her relationship with Austin had been progressing and getting more serious, and he was always complaining about not being able to spend enough time with her. Even though she explained the need for Do Not Disturb time to deal with the really brain-taxing things, he wanted in on that time. He said he just wanted to hang out in the same room as her. He wouldn't talk. He would just bring her coffee or lunch or rub her shoulders or give her an encouraging thumbs up.

Just the thought of someone constantly there during Do Not Disturb time, yanking her off her platform every few seconds, was enough to drive her mad. She dropped him like a hot potato.

She pulled into her garage, shut the door, and went into the kitchen at the back of the house so it wouldn't look like anyone was home. With headphones, she wouldn't even hear a knock on the door if one came. She settled into the room with the 1950s wallpaper that brought back the comfort of coming to visit Ammie as a child, and finally relaxed enough to get back on that platform and get everything done.

That was why she couldn't even entertain the thought of a relationship with Zane, no matter how attracted she was to him. Casual dating was fine because it never got to the "I even want to be with you when you're trying to deeply concentrate" stage.

But Zane wasn't someone she could ever imagine casual dating. She could only imagine going all-in with him, and that wasn't an option.

———

Alete piled her plate full of veggies as they were passed around her parents' dining room table which was always filled with happy chatter at their once-a-month family dinners. Between her, her parents, Ammie, her two brothers, one sister, their spouses, and her niece and two nephews, thirteen of them filled the space around the long oval table. This room and this table had felt gigantic when she was a little kid, but apparently, her parents knew clear back when they built the house that this was how it would one day be, so they planned for it.

They were to the "update everyone on what they've been doing over the past month" part of the dinner, and it came to Alete's turn. There was nothing that made her feel like she lived a boring life more than telling someone what she'd been up to. Especially after hearing her siblings talk about all the "firsts" her two nephews and her niece had accomplished.

"The hotel is going well. I hired a new high school kid to help Morgan in housekeeping, and he's working out great. We just had Fall Market last weekend. Um. I think that's it."

"That's not all," her dad said. "She's just being modest. She's also been helping the new Fire Chief and Emergency Management Director, Chief Collins, with some emergency preparedness things for the city."

She wasn't being modest; she just hadn't wanted it brought up. So she quickly added, "And my soccer team is good— after you all head back home today, we're going to get together for a night game."

"Oh," her brother, Nate, said. "I forgot to tell you. I signed us up for a sibling 'Debate the Movie' night. I was hoping you would come to Mountain Springs with us after dinner."

"Nate! You can't just control my time like that without even asking! Do you remember that guy I used to date— Steven? He planned my schedule without asking me all the time. I dumped him faster than Rob loses at Battleship."

"Hey," Rob said.

From the corner of her eye, she could see that her sister Talei was scrutinizing her. So she turned in her direction. "What?"

Talei gasped, and her hand flew to her chest. "You're interested in Chief Collins."

"What? No! I'm not. I'm not interested at all. Relationships cramp my style."

"As you've said for years," Talei said, and she fed little Dez a bite of peas. "But you always do this when you're interested in someone— you bring up annoying things that past boyfriends did. Like you're trying to talk yourself out of being interested in a new boyfriend. Which means you're interested!"

"If you only knew what a bull-headed, frustrating man Zane is, you wouldn't be saying that."

"Oh! First name basis," her brother, Rob, said. "I think that means she's interested *and* serious."

"We only get together once a month, yet you think you can guess everything."

Talei shook her head. "Not *everything*, obviously. That's where Ammie comes in." She turned to their grandma. "You know about this fire chief and Alete. I can tell by that sparkle in your eyes."

"I'm not saying a thing," Ammie said, zipping her lips. Taylor, Alete's two-year-old nephew who sat beside her, mimicked the motion, giggling like they shared the secret.

She was going to have to buy her grandma a caramel sundae for this.

Ammie unzipped her lips halfway, and, from the corner of her mouth, said, "I will say that he's very hot, though."

Her mom laughed the loudest, then got up to answer a knock at the door. At least that somewhat distracted everyone, and she was sure that the update was going to move on to her sister-in-law, Hope. To help signal that her update was done, she stabbed a spear of broccoli with her fork and put it in her mouth.

And then she nearly choked on the broccoli when her mom came back in the room with Zane at her side, Ranger next to him. "What are you doing here?"

"Alete!" her mom said. "That's no way to treat a guest who stopped by."

She swallowed her bite of broccoli. "I'm sorry. Hi. Welcome to my parents' house." She spread her arm, motioning at everyone around the table, using a mock-formal voice. "I'd like you to meet my family. Family, this is Chief Collins and his dog Ranger. What brings you by this evening?" She hoped that none of her siblings were watching her closely enough to tell that her heart rate had picked up and her stomach was fluttering.

Looking very uncomfortable at having so many pairs of eyes on him, Zane said, "I stopped by your house. When you didn't answer, your neighbor said you were three houses up and that I should come here. I just came by to say that we are at ninety percent."

"On the Go Bags?"

Zane nodded.

"Wow! So quickly?"

"Looks like everyone really wants to see us live-streaming our sleep deprivation."

"When?"

"When would you like to?"

"Aww, look at that!" Talei said. "He's even letting you set the date instead of controlling your time without asking."

Alete shot her sister the look that, as kids, they pretended shot lasers. Then she grabbed her phone off the side table and pulled up the calendar. "Saturday is covered by good people at the hotel. I could work on things to make sure the day is clear. How about Friday night into Saturday? That way we'll have Sunday to recover."

"Sounds good. I'll get it lined up."

"You haven't eaten, have you?" her mom asked. "You've got to join us."

Zane shifted his weight like he was preparing to turn and leave. "No, it's okay. Plus, I have Ranger with me."

But Alete's dad had already grabbed a chair and pushed it up to the table, and everyone already scooted their chairs to make room, and Talei was already getting up to get Ranger a bowl of water because her family never turned anyone away at dinner time.

"Sorry," Alete said. "If you show up here during dinner, you pretty much don't have a choice about leaving. This dining room is the Hotel California." She prayed that everyone wouldn't continue with the conversation they'd been having, since it had been all about Zane.

They didn't, but it was obvious by everyone's inability to start another conversation that their minds were still on this man who was now sitting at their table, looking like he wished he'd never followed her neighbor's advice to knock on Ed and Linda Keetch's door.

When Zane walked into the high school just a few minutes before ten p.m., a cooler in one hand and a bag with some supplies in the other, Alete was already waiting for him in the foyer.

"No Ranger?"

He shook his head. "No sense sleep-depriving an innocent dog. Stockton took him for the night."

"Are you ready for this?" Alete was almost bouncing on her toes with excitement. No matter how much excitement she managed to muster right now, he doubted she'd still be feeling that way before the night was over.

"You had a good amount of caffeine before coming, didn't you?"

She laughed and then held up her phone. "How about we start with a live video?" Alete had brought a tripod with her and attached her phone to it, then positioned it to where they could talk to the town with the Nestled Hollow High School logo and the Jimmy the Silver Miner mascot sculpture as a backdrop, and then she started the video.

"Hello, Nestled Hollow! Alete Keetch coming at you live with Emergency Management Director slash Fire Chief Zane Collins. We've both been up since six this morning. It's now ten p.m., and because you were all so incredible at getting your Go Bags ready and checking in on your neighbors, too, we have sequestered ourselves here for the next twelve hours without sleeping, and we'll be documenting exactly how this lack of sleep affects us."

"What do you say we start with a baseline?" Zane asked. He pulled out two bags of popcorn and handed one to Alete. "We are each going to try ten times to toss a piece of popcorn up in the air and catch it in our mouths. We'll see how we do with this challenge as the night goes on."

Alete moved closer to the phone and said, "I wanted us to toss grapes into our mouths, but our 'Safety First' Fire Chief wanted us to use something that was less of a choking hazard. That's how you know he's looking out for you, folks. He keeps you from choking."

"Ready?" he asked Alete. When she nodded, he said, "Go!" and they both started tossing pieces of popcorn in the air and trying to catch them. They only bumped into each other one time as they were both looking up and moving to get under their popcorn.

"Eight!" Alete shouted, her arms shooting straight up. "How many did you get, Mr. Safety?"

"Ten." Zane couldn't help the smile.

"You did not."

"See any pieces on the floor besides your two?"

Alete glanced around and then narrowed her eyes at him like she was trying to guess if he had tricked her. So Zane went straight up to the camera on the phone and said, "Dear viewers. Please tell us in the comments how many pieces you think I caught in my mouth."

Alete scooted in right next to him and said, "And tell us who you think is going to win the challenge at the one-third mark." Then, in a stage whisper, she said, "Psst. If you want to get the answer right, choose me."

Then they signed off and stopped the video streaming. This was one of the most exhilarating things he'd done in a while. He never would've done anything like it in Springvale. He never imagined he would do anything like this, anywhere, ever.

As the comments from Nestled Hollow residents poured in on their post, he realized he was starting to see that building a community— and not just a community among them, but a community with him included in it— made his job easier.

And how much he actually kind of enjoyed it. In

Springvale, he only dealt with people whose job was to comply with what he asked them to do. Here, he had to convince people to work with him. People who were busy with their own jobs and family and interests and had no obligation whatsoever to help. Maybe it really was time he fully joined this community.

"So," Alete said with her hands on her hips, looking at their surroundings. "What should we do now?"

10:47 P.M.

Alete started the live video on their community social media page and said, "High schoolers. Are you ever running late for class and wish you could just sprint through the hallways? You can live vicariously through me and the chief as we race our way through every hallway in the school."

She switched the camera to show in front of them, and Zane said, "Ready? Set..."

"Go!"

They both took off running down the hallways, cutting the corners as close as they could, pushing hard. Alete was fast. He should've known better than to think that it would be easy to win simply because he had the longer legs. He pushed himself harder every time he could tell she was pushing herself harder, the hallways whizzing by on their streaming video.

When they finally made it back to where they started,

both of them breathing heavily and pacing, hoping their heart rates would slow soon, Alete said to the camera between breaths, "I know it might've looked like a tie in that video, so you'll just have to trust me when I tell you that I won that one."

Zane poked his head into the frame. "Never trust someone who says the video lied. It was a tie."

11:33 P.M.

They had made their way to the atrium, an eight-sided room with floor-to-ceiling windows on six of the sides, and were sitting on one of the couches. Alete sat cross-legged and turned to face him, a bowl of grapes between the two of them. "Play This or That with me."

He turned to face her, too, one leg on the couch, bent. "This or That?"

She nodded. "One of us gives two choices, and you have to pick between the two. Then the other person goes. I'll start. Passenger or Driver?"

"Driver. Definitely."

"Driver for me, too. I guess if we ever go anywhere together, we'll have to battle it out."

Zane thought for a minute. "Facebook or Twitter?"

"Duh. Facebook. I'm guessing you'd choose Twitter?"

"Because it's a better way to get news. I'm guessing you chose Facebook because of the memes?"

"A *newspaper* is a better way to get news. Facebook is a

place to build community." Maybe she knew they could argue their points on this quite a bit, so she quickly said, "Laundry or Dishes?"

"Laundry. All you have to do is throw it in."

She nodded. "Agreed."

"Save or spend?"

Alete hesitated. "Mostly save. I mean obviously save for the things you want and save to be prepared. But then actually spend on the things you want."

That was more or less his philosophy, so he said, "Agreed."

"Hamburgers or tacos?"

He thought a moment and then said, "Hamburgers."

She looked at him like he was crazy. "Tacos! The answer is always tacos, Zane. No matter what the other option is, the correct answer is tacos."

He smiled at how passionate she got over something as simple as tacos. "Got it. Tacos. Okay, um...Oh! Dog or Cat."

"Cat."

"Wait, seriously? You'd choose to have a cat as a pet over having a dog?"

"No offense to Ranger."

"You don't like dogs?"

"I like dogs. I like when other people have dogs."

"Why? They greet you like you're the most amazing

person on the planet and act like they're so lucky to be in your presence."

She shrugged. "If you need that kind of reassurance, that's fine."

She said it with a gleam in her eye that told him she was teasing, but it still stung. "You've never had a dog, have you?"

"We had one when I was a kid."

"And you didn't love it with all your being? What kind of a person are you?"

"I'm just saying that I wouldn't want a pet who's always trying to be my best friend. I would want a pet like the roommate you never see until you cook a meal and they emerge, exchange a few pleasantries, and then go about their business."

He shook his head. He couldn't believe she was a cat person. He should've guessed after their first argument when she'd been such a pain. How could someone not prefer dogs? Maybe she was just giving that answer to get under his skin or to agree with him less.

"I just personally don't think dogs are the better pet."

"And I personally think you're wrong."

"We should ask our viewers." She turned on a livestream video and aimed it with both of them in the frame. "Zane— Chief Collins— and I were just having a discussion on which pet is better: cats or dogs."

"The answer is dogs, of course," Zane said.

"And I think the answer is cats. You should tell us what you think in the comments." Then she ended the video.

He just looked at her, shaking his head. "I guess you never really know a person until you have them answer the big questions."

She threw a grape at him.

1:12 A.M.

Zane and Alete had spent the better part of an hour grabbing items from different parts of the school and setting them up as an obstacle course in the gym.

They had standard school desks and chairs, all lying at various angles. They'd pulled over the mats that had been stacked against a wall in the gym and used some as padding to soften a landing and others folded as an obstacle. They grabbed a rolling chair out of a gym teacher's office. An ottoman from the atrium. A bench from the weight room. A few of the big exercise balls. The climbing rope that was attached to the ceiling.

For a moment, they'd thought about wheeling in one of the lunchroom tables, complete with the circle seats, but they decided maybe that would be a little too much.

They had arranged them into a course that went in a circle around the entire outer edge of the gym. Then they tried it, rearranged things, tried it again, and rearranged again. After a few more hunting trips through the school to find more objects, they finally had a course that was pretty amazing.

And Zane was having the most fun he'd had in a long time. How had he ever hoped that he would never see this woman again? She was bringing out a side of him that he hadn't known existed. Sometimes, like when she stood back and evaluated a section of the obstacle course to see if it was just right, he would just look at how perfect and full of energy and life she was and would start imagining what a life with her would be like.

But he'd had enough experiences in life to know that he couldn't trust anyone but himself. He had put up a shield to protect him from getting close to people a long time ago because he knew what would happen if the shield wasn't there.

And because he was so good at protecting people, himself included, it was an extremely solid shield. So in those moments when he was admiring her the most, he'd just remind himself that they disagreed on the important things.

Like dogs.

When they got back to the beginning of the obstacle course, her face was shining with excitement. "Are you ready?"

He nodded, so she turned on the live video and cleared her throat. "Check this out, Nestled Hollow. Zane and I have made the world's greatest obstacle course, and we are now about to time each other to see who can go through the course the fastest. Now we're only a couple of hours into our sleep deprivation, so we figure we're not to the point where we'll be a danger to ourselves yet."

"And since I lost the coin toss," Zane said, "I'm going first."

"Wait. Before you do, one more 'This or That' question. Precision or Speed?"

He smiled a little. "I'm pretty sure that the answer is tacos."

Alete laughed a loud, unrestrained, hearty laugh that made him chuckle. Then she pulled up the timer on his phone and showed it to the camera on hers. "Ready, set, go!"

Zane took off through the obstacle course, jumping over and around and through and under and between all the obstacles, racing quickly around each of the features they had set up. He finished on one of the long, spread-out mats, sliding to the end, feet first, as Alete stopped the timer.

She held it up to the camera. "And Zane finishes with a time of forty-two-point-three seconds. Everyone cheer for Zane by posting your favorite cheering gif in the comments!"

Zane caught his breath, then took both phones from Alete and reset the timer. "Before Alete goes, I think we better ask her the 'This or That' question. So, Alete, Speed or Precision?"

She gave the camera a playful smile. "Whatever it takes to win."

When he gave the word to go and he started the timer, Alete took off like she was racing for her life. He had done plenty of obstacle courses in many training sessions throughout his life as a firefighter. He doubted she had done any as the owner of a hotel, yet the woman's speed and agility were incredible.

During many of their practice runs, they were both trying it out at the same time, and he hadn't stopped to watch her. He knew she liked playing sports, and he could tell by looking at her that she ate healthy, but he was still blown away at how quickly and skillfully she was completing each part of the course.

He was glad he had the camera aimed only at her because he was sure he was watching in obvious slack-jawed amazement. At least he came out of his stupor in time to stop the timer when she reached the finish line. He turned the camera to himself as he held up the timer next to his astonished face. "Thirty-five-point-zero seconds, everyone. When you come out of your shocked stupor at the amazing feat of athleticism you just witnessed, make sure you give it up for Alete in the comments."

Then he turned the camera back to her as she stood with her hands on her hips, breathing heavily, a smile spread across her face, before he ended the live-stream video.

2:14 A.M.

After adjusting the phone on the tripod, Zane started the live-stream video. "And we are back! We are a little late with our one-third of the way through popcorn test because it took us quite a while to get all the items from our obstacle course put away. Now it's time to see just how badly the lack of sleep is affecting us. Are you ready, Alete?"

She bounced from one foot to the other, like she was about to run a race. "I was born ready!"

They threw their popcorn pieces in the air, one at a time, trying to catch them. When they had both finished, Alete said, "I definitely saw you miss a few this time. How many did you get?"

"Eight. You?"

"Zane! You weren't supposed to get that many!"

"How many did you get?"

"Seven."

Zane gave her the most innocent-looking smile he could manage, then said, "You probably lost because you're a cat person," before turning off the video.

3:37 A.M.

"I'm feeling loopy," Alete said as she leaned back in the

office chair and put her feet up on the filing cabinet. They had just raced down the halls on the wheeled chairs from the front office in an attempt to stave off extreme tiredness and were now back in the office.

Zane put his feet up on the filing cabinet, too. "That's the sleeplessness. In one of my college classes, my professor said that they did a study where they tested people who were overly drowsy and their reactions were the same as someone who was drunk."

"I believe it. That's how I feel. I mean I've never actually been drunk, but I'm guessing this is what it feels like."

"You've *never* been drunk?"

"Nope."

She paused a minute, then said, "Oh, I know what we can do. Drunk confessions. Except they're actually really tired confessions."

He raised an eyebrow. That didn't sound good. "What do you have in mind?"

"You tell me a story about you, and I tell you one about me. But it has to be something you wouldn't tell if you weren't sleep deprived."

The more time he spent with Alete, the more he wanted to know about her. He knew he shouldn't; learning more about her was dangerous to his shield, but it was so late and he couldn't seem to care enough to stop himself from wanting to hear whatever story she was willing to tell. "Okay, but only if you go first."

She scrutinized his expression like she was judging whether he was going to try to get out of his confession if she went first.

"Scout's honor," he said, saluting.

"Deal, then. What story do you want me to tell?"

He studied her, trying to figure out what to ask. Did he want to hear about past relationships? Just wondering made him realize how much he really did not. She probably went to this high school. Did he want to hear about that? He wished he could see all the stories in her head so he would know which one to pick.

"Tell me something from your childhood. Something that really defined who you are." He thought it would be a hard question that she'd have to think about for a while, but she seemed to already know what that something was.

"That's not a fun story."

"Hey, I'm not the one who has to have everything be fun."

She rolled her eyes, but just like when she'd done it to her grandma, it came across as playful. Maybe she couldn't pull off an annoyed or sarcastic eye roll.

"All right. When I was eleven, I was diagnosed with cancer."

He didn't hide the shock that he was sure showed on his face. "That's terrible."

"Yep. I mean, I was one of the lucky ones. Almost exactly a year after I was first diagnosed, I had my first scan that showed I was cancer free. A lot of kids I knew from the hospital had to fight for *years*. Several lost the fight."

She stood up and moved to lean against a windowsill. "It was awful. For a year, every single thing I did was dictated by someone or something else. I felt like I had no control over anything. Zero choices. With doctor's visits, chemo, radiation, tests, blood draws, IVs, hospital stays, getting deathly ill just because someone had walked past me who had a cold and I had no immune system, being tired all the time, my body giving out when I wanted to do things— all my time was spoken for.

"But I could still dream. And as I was lying in bed, too sick or too tired to get up, or as I was missing school and friends and soccer and being normal, I dreamed about the day when I would be past all of it. When cancer would just be a memory.

"And I decided that when I got to that point, I was going to live life differently than I had been. I was going to eat healthily and exercise so my body would always be the opposite of how it had been with cancer. Chemo wrecks your body, and it kind of makes you never want to put anything harmful into your body ever again.

"That's why I don't drink. I was going to pack my life as full of all the things I wanted to do as I could. And I wasn't ever going to let something or someone else dictate where I'd spend my time, and I was going to spend it doing important things.

"I had lots of support as I was going through all of it. My parents, my siblings, Ammie and my grandpa Erickson, my grandparents on my dad's side, everyone in my class at school, and a whole bunch of Nestled Hollow angels. So I decided that those 'important things' I was going to spend my time doing was helping the people who live here to feel the same sense of community I felt as I was going through cancer treatments."

He couldn't stand to see kids hurting or in pain, and hearing about her going through cancer treatments at such a young age hurt. Like he'd been stabbed in his heart. The whole story made him respect her even more. "That's...wow. So tough."

"Do you know what, though? It's okay. At first, I'll admit that I felt picked on by life because of it. But it didn't take long to be able to look back and see that I wouldn't be the person I am today without it, and I kind of like the person I am."

He kind of liked the person she was, too. And that scared him more than running into a building on fire ever had.

ALETE

"You don't want to share?" Alete said, following Zane out of the office and into the lobby. "You can't just go back on our deal."

He turned around. "How am I supposed to follow that story? I mean, childhood cancer? That's a mic drop right there. I can't just pick up the mic and tell a story about me without it making me a jerk."

She crossed her arms. "The only way you'd be a jerk is if you chose not to tell your story. You promised you would. 'Scout's honor.' If you now go back on your promise, karma will probably make you get run over by a car while crossing the street." She sat down cross-legged at the foot of Jimmy the Silver Miner just to show she wasn't going anywhere. "I can wait patiently. Or, if you prefer, I can visit you in the hospital after you get hit by that car."

He huffed, but then sat down opposite her, cross-legged, too, but leaning back on his hands. "Okay. What story would you like me to tell?"

"Let's do the same. Something from your childhood that really defined who you are."

"My childhood was not particularly enjoyable and not all that interesting."

"Even if it wasn't, I'm sure you can come up with an interesting nugget to share."

He stayed quiet for several long moments, but he didn't look like he was getting closer to knowing what he wanted to talk about.

"You mentioned the dog from your childhood. Oliver, right?" He seemed impressed and maybe a little pleased that she had remembered. "Tell me that story."

"Okay, I can do that. Well, Oliver really was the best dog and had the softest golden brown fur. My parents were gone all the time on cruises or traveling the world or going on business trips, so they got me Oliver in hopes that he would be a good substitute for their presence.

"He was the greatest. He would snuggle up to me when I had to go to bed when no one was home. He would sit down right on my lap if I was ever scared. Lick my face if I was ever sad. Play ball if I ever wanted someone to do something with."

"And he reminded you about everything that was important."

He chuckled softly. "You remembered. Yeah, he was good at that." His face was lit up and seemed so much more relaxed and happy when he was talking about Oliver. "And he was good around other people, too. I would take him to the park and if little kids came over—even if it was a lot of little kids— he would never freak out. He would rub his nose into their outstretched hands, and they loved it and he loved it. He was no guard dog, but he sure protected me."

At hearing his voice turn sad, she whispered, "What happened to him?"

He looked up at Jimmy the Silver Miner for a long minute, but like he wasn't really seeing him. She held her breath, hoping he would continue, yet knowing that there probably wouldn't have opened up like this if it hadn't been for the sleep deprivation.

Finally, he said, "I got Oliver when I was nine, not long after my parents stopped hiring an adult to stay with us when they went on their trips. They figured that my fourteen-year-old brother was old enough to take care of us, but my brother seemed more interested in the lack of a curfew, being able to spend unlimited time with his friends, and getting into trouble than he was in taking care of me.

"That was also right around the time that I started really worrying that something was going to happen to us. Especially because my brother was not good at making sure the doors to our house were locked at night. Even when my parents were home, they weren't great at it, either.

"So, at age nine, I took on that responsibility myself. I saw it as my job to protect my family because nobody else was."

"Wow. That's young." His face shone with a sense of sadness from long ago, and she wanted to reach out and put a hand on his arm, his shoulder, his cheek. Something to comfort him. "So you've had this drive to protect people since you were little, then."

"For as long as I can remember. I was a little kid, so I had to go to bed before my brother usually came home, and when my parents were in town but out with friends or having friends over for drinks, before them. So when I went to bed, I tried to not fall asleep too deeply so I could hear when they came home.

"Then, one day when I was thirteen, I was recovering from a bad cold, and I fell asleep too deeply and didn't get up to lock the doors after my brother came home. That night, someone broke into our house. Well, they didn't exactly 'break in'— they just walked right into our unlocked house.

"And I didn't hear a single thing. But Oliver, being the friendly dog he was, must've gone in to see what the noise was, and probably made friends with the thieves as easily as he made friends with anyone.

"They stole some cash, a laptop, our TV, and my dog. What kind of person steals a little kid's dog? I mean, he was the world's greatest dog, and he was pretty hard to resist. But that was tough."

Now she understood why his need to make sure everyone was protected was so strong. He was probably trying to make up for not having protected his dog from the people who robbed his house. She blinked away the tears that were forming in her eyes because she knew that wouldn't make him having shared that story any easier on him.

"You know it wasn't your fault he was stolen, right?"

He shrugged.

"It *wasn't* your fault," she said more forcefully. "And even though they should've definitely taken better care of you, it wasn't your brother's fault, and it wasn't your parents' fault, either. Oliver getting stolen was the fault of the thieves themselves."

"I get that. I do. But it doesn't mean I was powerless."

"Ahh. I understand. If Nestled Hollow had a natural disaster, it wouldn't be your fault, but you know you aren't powerless to help. So that's what drives you."

They met eyes for a long moment, and she felt a profound appreciation coming from Zane for her understanding.

Then she said, "Wow, Zane. Your story is a bigger mic drop than my cancer story."

He chuckled, shook his head, and then she let him pull her to her feet.

5:02 A.M.

Alete could barely keep her eyes open and her head felt too heavy to hold up. Zane sat close to her on the couch in the atrium where they had been playing cards, so she leaned against him, resting her head against his shoulder. "I'm so tired. So, so tired." She closed her eyes. "I just need to sleep for a little bit."

"Alete, you can't." Zane tried to nudge her upright, but she didn't have the energy.

"Just for a little bit. I swear it won't be long." She reached out and ran her hand down his upper arm. "Your shirt is so soft. And your arm is so nice. Great for sleeping on. Like a firm, supportive mattress."

"Alete."

"Isn't it strange how, when you spend so many hours during the middle of the night with a person, it makes it feel like you've known them forever? Doesn't it feel like we've known each other forever? Like I could tell you anything."

"I think you're delirious."

"I think I'm sleepy."

"I know what we should do." Zane nudged her a little more firmly. "We haven't done a video for the community page in a while. We already ran through the school.

What do you think about sneaking through it in the dark?"

This time she did sit up at least a little more straight. And it gave her brain a little tiny nudge to start working again. "Like we're hunting for ghosts?"

"Sure. We can go with that."

"That would be cool. Like a spook alley."

They both stood up, and Zane started the live video from his phone. "Okay, folks, it's now a little after five a.m. and we've decided to take you on a spooky tour of what the school looks like in the pre-dawn hours. Because if we don't, Alete here is going to fall asleep, and I know she doesn't want to disappoint you all."

She nodded her head and then felt like that was the wrong answer and shook her head. "I don't."

Zane switched the camera to show what was in front of them as they walked toward the lobby at the front of the school. Emergency lights were on there, so even though it was darker than normal, it wasn't exactly spooky. It only got dark when they headed down the classroom hallways. She wrapped both arms around one of Zane's, holding on tightly. "See any ghosts?"

"Not yet."

She didn't remember these hallways ever being so creepy. It was just so dark, and the light that filtered in from the emergency lights or from streetlights outside shining through the windows only made it feel spookier.

"I heard that the old Nestled Hollow High had ghosts before they tore it down. But most of them went home or something and only Jimmy came to this school because he likes that there's a statue of him here."

"Is that so?"

"Probably not. But if he is here, you'd think we'd see him, right?"

"I'm sure we would."

She could hear the smile in his voice, and part of her knew that she wasn't exactly being logical, but it felt like her brain wasn't fully connected.

"Oh, the science lab!" She pulled Zane toward it. "When Mr. Hawkins was in this room, he had a gecko, a bird that squawked at everyone, a big snake that he fed mice to, and jars full of all kinds of creepy things like you'd see in a spook alley."

When they got there, Alete pulled back from the doorway, suddenly unsure that she actually wanted to see them in a dark school in the middle of the night, and said, "I'm scared. You first."

Zane, being the brave protector that he was, squared his shoulders even more, and aimed the camera ahead, looking through the tall skinny window in the door at the lab beyond. "Okay, Nestled Hollow, we're about to see what the science lab looks like in the dark."

Suddenly feeling a little more awake and a lot less

scared now with Zane between her and the science lab, Alete quietly slipped back behind a pillar in the hallway.

"Locked," Zane said, and then, "Alete?" A little louder, "Alete?"

She waited until the count of three, and then jumped out from behind the pillar, yelling a guttural sound, her arms raised. Zane dropped the phone that they'd been recording the live video on as he stepped a foot back into a defensive stance, fisted hands up and ready for action until he saw it was just her, and then dropped them to his sides.

Alete laughed so loudly that it woke her up the rest of the way. She leaned down and picked up the phone and aimed the camera at herself. "A couple of months ago, the day that Chief Collins moved to Nestled Hollow, he came into All Nestled Inn and scared me. At that point, we found out that I react to danger by dropping whatever I'm holding and flinching enough to nearly fall off my ladder. And now we know how Chief Collins reacts."

She was still chuckling at how effective her jump scare was—she hadn't anticipated it working nearly that well.

"So if you ever need protecting, he's your guy. It was impressive, Chief, how quickly you responded to danger. I guess in a fight, flight, or freeze scenario, we can count on you to fight." The hallways were dark, but in the faint light, she thought she detected a bit of a blush on his cheeks. "Signing off for now."

Alete was still chuckling, her heart still racing from the adrenaline, her senses alive from being so awake after being so sleepy. And then she noticed the way that Zane was looking at her— like he was seeing her and understanding her, and it made her heart race even more. Possibly because she was seeing him differently than she had before, too.

Maybe she had been seeing him differently for a while. Or maybe tonight really had been the equivalent of knowing each other forever.

He took a step closer to her, and she stepped closer, too. She held his phone out, and he took it from her, his fingers brushing against her hand as he did, and she found herself closing her eyes and soaking in the light touch.

"I like you, Alete."

She smiled, looking up at his beautiful face in the faint light. "I like you, too, Zane." The words felt so pedestrian — not nearly eloquent enough for the emotions swirling in her. Maybe eloquence wasn't meant to come after being awake for more than twenty-three hours.

"Do you think it's possible for two people who disagree on so much to ever work out as a couple?"

The words were so bold, yet it gave her such a thrill to say "a couple."

He raised an eyebrow. Such a little motion, but it brought with it a gleam in his eye that promised possibilities of future joy and prosperity. A joy and prosperity that right now, she really wanted in her future. "I mean, we don't *always* disagree."

"That's true," she said. "Sometimes you just accept that I'm right from the start."

Zane laughed, and the sound rumbled through the empty hallway. A sound she could really get used to. "You know that just makes me want to disagree with you more, right?"

He took a step toward her, his eyes not leaving hers, and as sleepy as she had been when she'd said that this night made it feel like they had known each other forever instead of weeks, she felt it deeply now that she was more awake, her senses on high alert. She closed the gap between them even more so that only a breath of space was between them. "So, if I said that I think we should start dating, you'd disagree on principle?"

He chuckled and ran his hand down her arm and entwined his fingers in hers. "That's a tough one. I think I'd have to agree, as much as it's in my nature to do otherwise."

"Wow, Chief Collins agrees with Alete. I think we need that cross-stitched and hung in a frame at the fire station. Now, tell me, Chief, if I said, 'I think we should kiss,' would you be inclined to agree with me a second time? In the same minute, even?"

He smiled that amused smile, the one that made his lips curve up on the one side, dimpling his cheek, his eyes shining. Then he put his hand on the small of her back and brought her even closer. "You caught me on a good day. I'm feeling rather agreeable."

He glanced at her lips once before closing the space between them and pressing his lips against hers, sure and unwavering. She closed her eyes and let go of his hand, wrapping her arms around his neck as he cupped his now free hand at the back of her neck, his fingers tangling in her hair.

She pressed her lips against his, the two of them moving their lips in time with each other, his lips smooth, his motions confident. She breathed in the scent of him, the feel of him, the rightness of him.

Her stomach fluttered at finally having this man so close to her, his lips on hers, and not "accidentally." There was nothing accidental about this. It felt like she'd been waiting a lifetime for it.

He moved his kisses along her jawline, barely touching the skin, causing tingles to go up her spine and neck. She ran her fingers across those strong, sure shoulders. When his lips got to her ear, he whispered, "You were right."

"I agree," she whispered back. "What was I right about?"

"That it was a good idea to kiss."

She let out a contented sigh. "It was an excellent idea."

Her stomach growled, long and loud, and she felt Zane smile as he kissed her cheek. Why hadn't she guessed that she would need food during these hours if she wasn't going to be sleeping? And why, oh why, did her stomach have to interrupt their kiss to let them know about her oversight?

Zane took a step back from her and placed his hand in hers. "They teach culinary classes here, right? How about we go make breakfast."

"You brought stuff to make breakfast?"

"Preparedness is my middle name."

"You weren't just a Boy Scout— you earned your Eagle, didn't you?"

"By the time I was fourteen. First one in my troop."

As they cooked breakfast on one of the student cooking stations, the smell of pancakes, bacon, eggs, and fresh fruit woke her up, giving her more energy and clearing her brain fog. And made her realize just how great Zane looked, even when cooking breakfast after being awake for nearly twenty-four hours, even when her brain was feeling more Alete-like.

And it might have possibly made her imagine what life with Zane might be like. They had spent eight hours straight together, and she still wasn't ready to unlock a door and toss him out like she thought she'd be after about two hours. That had to be some kind of record for her.

5:58 A.M.

With her camera on the tripod, she started a live-stream video and said it was time for their two-thirds-of-the-way-through popcorn test. She was so glad they were doing it after eating breakfast and not closer to five a.m. when she'd been so sleepy. If they had done it then, she'd have looked like a fool and only gotten one, if she was lucky. And Zane probably would've still gotten most of his.

But since she was back to feeling like she was awake and alert, she really concentrated and tried hard. "Yes! I got seven! Pretty impressive for twenty-four hours awake. How'd you do?"

"Seven as well."

"Well, that's not exactly a win in my column, but, Nestled Hollow, I think you'll agree that we're both pretty darn impressive."

She shut off the camera, and Zane tossed a piece of popcorn in the air in her direction, and she caught it and shot both arms into the air. "I wish we would've gotten that on camera!"

As she unhooked her phone from the tripod, thinking about how much she had enjoyed being around him, he asked, "Football or Basketball?" and it took her a minute to realize what he was asking.

"Playing? Both. Watching? Football. Winter or Summer?"

"Winter," Zane said. "It makes the heat of firefighting more bearable. Netflix or YouTube?"

"YouTube."

Zane made a show of studying her. "It's because of the cat videos, isn't it?"

"It's because I'm not going to sit there long enough to watch an entire show. Put Down Roots or Wanderlust?"

"Wanderlust."

"Wait, really?"

He nodded. "There are lots of cities that need an Emergency Management Director with experience. I'm hoping to get a state capitol someday."

"You're not planning to stay in Nestled Hollow?"

"Not forever." He didn't let her dwell on that long, though, before saying, "Go Out or Stay at Home?"

She answered "Go out," but her mind didn't fully let go of the fact that Zane was planning to leave when his work here was done. She hadn't expected news like that would distress her— not long ago it would've made her do a happy dance— but now it was hitting her hard, and she didn't quite know how to process that information. She grasped for any question and came up with, "Big Crowd or Small Group?"

"Small group."

She narrowed her eyes at him. "Is that why you don't want us to have town celebrations?"

"Alete," he said, his shoulders dropping. "It's not that I don't want you to have them. It's that we need the money to get Nestled Hollow prepared for disaster."

"And who says it's even going to stop there? Getting a

town prepared isn't just a one-time event— it's continual. I'm sure next year will come along and you'll want the money all over again for all the things you couldn't buy this time."

"I only plan to take it this year."

She wasn't sure she believed it would only be a one-time thing, though, especially if he didn't see the value in town events. "Oh! I've got an idea. We have a captive audience right now. We've gotten so many comments, and I'm sure even more will pour in as people start waking up. How about we live-stream another video and ask the town what they think? We could do a poll to see if people would rather buy equipment or continue our town traditions with the festivals we have planned."

"You can't ask them!"

"Why not?"

"Because they'll never choose what's best. That'd be like asking a kid if he would rather have a regular meal or candy for dinner."

She could feel the heat rising at the base of her neck, and she really didn't want to disagree with him. Especially not after all they had shared. But knowing how he really felt about her town stung. "I guess now I understand why you want to get out of here as soon as you can."

"Alete, I didn't mean it like that. I wasn't knocking Nestled Hollow—I was just referring to human nature in general. It's hard to commit resources to something that isn't flashy, especially when it's something that you hope will never be needed."

She understood that. She wanted her town to be prepared; they just disagreed on how much should be spent on it this year.

And it made her think that her parents wouldn't have this disagreement. They probably wouldn't have disagreed on anything all night, yet she and Zane had found just as much to disagree on as agree. She had started to let herself imagine a life with Zane, so it was good to get that reminder that they didn't see eye-to-eye on everything.

He stepped closer and wrapped his arms around her, the motion instantly starting to calm her. She had imagined his arms around her so many times but hadn't ever imagined that it would feel so right.

"We both have pretty strong opinions, and I'm sure we'll find plenty of things to debate. But I don't want that to put a wedge between us. Maybe we should just agree to leave the work stuff at work. We can discuss it all we want then and leave it behind when we're not at work. I like you way too much not to try."

"I'd like that," she said and leaned her head against his chest. She would much rather spend this moment memorizing how it felt to be in Zane Collins's arms.

nineteen

ZANE

Zane grabbed two CPR dummies out of his truck and carried them, one under each arm, into the elementary school and down the hall to the classroom where the CPR class would be taught.

He glanced at the clock— it was now twelve-fifteen. He and his crew were putting on a three-hour event that would run from one to four, and Alete had said she'd be there at noon to help set up and run the event. He took his phone off his belt clip to make sure he hadn't missed a call or text from her saying why she was late.

Nothing.

A part of Zane had worried that his kiss with Alete in the hallway of the high school, along with their decision to date, wasn't going to sound so wise after a good night's sleep. That it had all been a product of sleep deprivation.

But he woke up the next morning feeling refreshed and even more excited to be dating Alete.

In the two weeks since their all-nighter, they had been texting off and on all day and calling each other before going to bed each night, talking long into the night. They had gone out to eat a few times at Nestled Hollow restaurants, he had invited her for lunches he cooked at the fire station kitchen a couple of times, and he had even joined in on her weekly soccer game until a call came in and he had to leave early.

They had kept town issues out of their conversations, and had just enjoyed getting to know each other. Daily as he lay down to bed at night, he found he had fallen for her more than he had the night before.

In their sign-off video at the end of their all-nighter, when they had done their final popcorn test and lessons learned about their experiment, the town seemed to sense that things had changed between the two of them. Speculations in the comments section ran rampant—something that, weeks ago, or even last week, he would've expected to drive him nuts. But somehow, it hadn't bothered him. Somehow, it felt like the town was just cheering them on. And since he wanted him and Alete to win with their relationship, it felt like they were on his side.

But by ten minutes to one, the elementary school gym was filled with people, and Alete still hadn't shown up, texted, or called. He wondered if she forgot. Or if something better came up.

Even though he tried to push the thoughts away, all his old, familiar fear kept poking its way in. Fear that he couldn't trust anyone to be there for him because they would always let him down. He kept having flashbacks to growing up with his parents. They would always say they were going to come to the things that were important to him, and they always had a really good excuse after as to why they didn't show up.

A couple of minutes before it started, his entire crew came up to the front with him. They all stood in a line, not only in uniform but with uniformly shaved heads. All of them had ended up getting in on the head-shaving experience— even Amy got part of her head shaved after being so adamant that no one was going to come near her with shavers.

He liked that they supported the cause. But at the same time, as he stood with them as the only one who hadn't gotten his head shaved, it made him feel like an outsider, even among his own crew.

He mouthed, "All set?" to his crew, and they gave him thumbs up, so he cleared his throat and stepped up to the microphone. "Thank you all for spending your Saturday afternoon here. We're glad to have you, and we think that by the time you leave, you'll be feeling more prepared and be glad you came. We have several classes for you, and my crew is excited to teach the things they're experts on.

"We are going to start by going to the parking lot just outside these doors, so keep your jackets close. We've got part of a kitchen we made from items we found at the dump, and it's all sitting on plywood. I'm going to show you what happens when you pour water on a kitchen fire and what happens when you pour baking soda on it. Then I'll show you how to use a fire extinguisher.

"Then we'll head back inside. All of you who are ten years old and younger, raise your hand. You'll be staying in this room, and these two guys, Judah and Liam, along with their helpers are going to run a safety first fair for you right in this room. Give me thumbs up if you've got it."

He smiled when all the little kids raised their thumbs.

"Okay, everyone ages eleven to...who's the oldest one here?"

A woman in the back yelled out "Me! I'm ninety-three!"

"Wow! Nice job on the aging to you! Okay, everyone ages eleven to ninety-three, you can choose to go to any of the classes, including the safety fair in this room."

It struck him how much more at ease he was as he spoke to a big crowd like this than when he first came to Nestled Hollow. He was sure it was mostly Alete's doing. He wondered again where she might be.

"We've got a CPR class, where Amy will teach you

some of her best EMT skills in the fifth-grade classroom. Tila," he said and paused while Tila raised her hand, "is teaching a class in the library on babysitting and what to do if there's an emergency while you're taking care of little ones. Legacy, another of our EMTs, is teaching basic first aid in the fourth-grade classroom. Jim will be doing radio communications in the teacher's lounge.

"In about a month, we are going to do the full twenty-hour Community Emergency Response Team— or CERT — training. If any of you think you might be interested, Jarred is going to run a mini course that we hope will get you excited to do the full course. Stockton has even come out of his retirement to assist Jarred.

"And then we have our brand new incident command trailer on display at the back of the gym. Anyone staying in this room will get a chance to see it as one of the activities here, but everyone else, make sure you come by sometime today to check it out."

He was so proud of what he'd been able to get with the budget they had, and he couldn't wait for them to see it. "Alright, everyone, pick your class and head there now!"

Zane spent the next three hours giving his demonstration outside, then going from class to class, checking in on them, and worrying about Alete. He had enough crew and volunteers for everything to run smoothly, so it wasn't a huge deal that she hadn't shown up, but he wanted to see her.

He texted her once, asking if she was planning to come, and hadn't gotten a response. He started the event being worried about her, but as it was winding down, he let the thought in that had been hovering for three hours —that it hadn't mattered enough to her. That he hadn't mattered enough. Just like with his parents.

As the classes finished and the parents headed back to the gym to pick up their kids and check out the incident command trailer, Zane hung out in the gym, answering questions. Just as he finished talking with an older gentleman who was concerned about what to do with his twelve cats if they ever had to be evacuated, he heard a younger family walk up to Stockton, who was standing just a few feet away. "You put on a great event today, Chief."

"Actually, it was Chief Collins—"

"Right," the man said, turning to Zane and nodding. "Chief Collins. Good to see you." Then the man turned back to Stockton and said. "Anyway, we all really enjoyed it. I went to the first aid class, Sue went to CPR, and my kiddos both stayed in here and loved it. Nice work today."

Zane ground his teeth. None of them had even gone to the CERT class where Stockton was, so it wasn't like they were thanking him for the class he helped with. It felt like Springvale all over again, where the Emergency Management Director got credit for everything Zane did.

As the family walked away, Stockton turned to Zane.

"Sorry about that. You know people. They're slow to accept change— they didn't mean anything by it."

He tried to let the annoyance roll off his shoulders because Alete had just stepped through the doorway into the gym and was walking over to him. So at least he knew she hadn't been in an accident or something.

"I'm so sorry," she said as she closed the last few feet. "Ammie got vertigo that wouldn't go away with the normal tricks and her whole world was spinning. My parents were in Boulder visiting my brother Nate, so I had to take her to the hospital."

So she had been dealing with an emergency. He felt bad that a part of him felt better at this news. "Is she okay?"

"She is now. But you know emergency rooms. They make you wait forever."

He'd felt better until her last sentence. "You were waiting forever, and you couldn't take a moment to at least text to let me know that you couldn't be here?"

She flinched. "I'm sorry."

After all the stress and work that went into pulling off this event, and how much time he'd spent worrying about her and being upset with her and wondering if she was just blowing him off, all she was going to offer was "Sorry?"

He shook his head in bewilderment. "Letting someone know that you can't make it to something you committed to is just common courtesy, Alete." It was harsh and he knew it, but he was so upset that she didn't seem to care about this.

Her eyes held that same fierceness that he loved when it wasn't negatively aimed at him, and he instantly knew he had pushed too far. "First, you text me saying, 'I could use help on Saturday from noon to four. Can I count on you to be there?' Now, normally I would say no to anyone who planned my time for me like that and just expected me to be there, but I gave you a pass because of how much I care about you. But Zane? This is not my job. I'm not getting paid for this, which means I don't have to put up with you treating me like you're the boss or like I'm the enemy."

He was opening his mouth, already forming the apology, when Alete's eyes fell on the incident command trailer. "You already bought it?"

"Yeah. It just came in yesterday, so we got it all loaded up and have been showing everyone today. They've all been really impressed..." The words died as he saw the expression on her face. She definitely wasn't as excited about it as the rest of the town had been.

"And even after everything— after knowing how I feel about town events, and experiencing firsthand what they do to bring this town together as a community, you took that money from five town festivals? You took it from *my* festival?"

"But I've given you extra town bonding events, like the

Go Bag scavenger hunt and the block parties. Now, I am sure that the Thankful for You festival is great. I'm not saying I want to end it. As I said, it's just for one year."

"Zane, it doesn't work that way! I have been over this event for the past six years. And it's only been a thing for ten. In my first year, we only had forty people show up. Last year, we had nine hundred. *Nine hundred*. That only happened because I worked hard and people grew to know what to expect and trusted the event. If we cancel, I doubt we could get more than two hundred the next year. It would be almost like starting over; years of hard work would just be gone."

"This town knows you better now than they knew you at twenty-two. It won't take as long to get the numbers back up."

She threw her arms up and turned away like she wasn't even willing to look in his direction. A lot of the people had already left or were wrapped up in their own conversations in groups in the gym, only occasionally looking at them to see what was going on.

He needed Alete to understand. He walked toward her, forcing his voice to come out calm, and said, "This equipment is vital to this town's safety. I've looked, Alete. I've tried to find money in other places, but that was the only option. I wish it wasn't. I wish I could tell you that you could keep your festivals, especially the Thankful for You one."

She turned back around, seemingly willing to listen, so he added, "The equipment is just more important than your festivals."

The moment the words came out, he knew he shouldn't have said them. He knew it even without the look of hurt, anger, disbelief, and disappointment on Alete's face.

Alete stepped closer to him, her eyes searching his. "The worst part," she whispered, "is that you didn't even trust me enough to tell me. You knew I was still hoping to figure out a way to have the festival. You should've told me the money was already gone."

He wanted to say that he hadn't brought it up because they had agreed not to talk about work when they weren't at work, but the excuse was flimsy, and he knew it. Their opinions and the things that were important to them didn't change just because they didn't talk about them.

"I can't do this, Zane." She turned and walked out of the gym, a finality about it that felt like she was taking a part of him with her.

More than two months ago, when he had first argued with her at the combined Main Street Business Alliance and city council meeting, he would've felt like he'd won if he got her to back out of everything to do with his job as Emergency Management Director.

Now, though, all he felt was an immense loss.

ALETE

When Alete got back to her parents' house, she heard a lot of strange sounds and what she feared was wailing from her grandma. She hurried to unlock the door and found her grandma sitting on the recliner, watching TikTok videos of little kids being funny.

"Ammie! I thought you were hurt!"

"Nope. Just laughing," she said, followed quickly by another round of howling laughter.

"I thought you were going to take a nap while I ran to the elementary school."

"But then I thought that laughter has more healing power than sleep, so I figured watching these is better than medicine." Then she glanced at Alete and said, "Oh," and paused the video on a kid holding an avocado. "It went that poorly?"

Alete was still fuming from all the things Zane had said, and the drive back to her parents' house hadn't calmed her— it just made all the frustration ready to burst out of her. "He was so rude, Ammie! It's like all he cares about is whatever is important to him at the moment and anything that is going on with anybody else doesn't matter."

"I'm sorry I made you miss the event."

"*No*, Ammie. You are more important than that event, and *some* people need to remember that. He just makes me so angry! I mean, first, he thinks he's the boss of this town, and then the boss of my time. Well, he's not the boss of the town and he's definitely not the boss of me."

"So what did you tell him?"

Alete paced back and forth. Three steps one way, three steps the other, then she'd stop because more needed to be said, then do it all over again. "I told him that he could take his event and throw it in the lake."

"Really."

"No, not really. I told him that I am done, and I walked away. Why should I care about the things he wants everyone to do when he doesn't care about the things I want everyone to do?" She groaned in frustration. "He makes me crazy!"

She forced herself to stop pacing because she was probably making her grandma nauseous. "Why aren't you picking up your metaphorical pitchfork? Or telling me to go kick him in the shins?"

Ammie sat in silence for a long moment while Alete tried to patiently wait.

Instead of getting mad on her behalf, Ammie said, "Any guesses why you're feeling so angry toward him?"

Alete opened her mouth to list some more reasons, but she knew that wasn't what her grandma was asking. She let out a long breath and dropped to a seat on the couch. "Yes. Because I don't actually hate him; I love him. But Ammie! I didn't want to admit that!"

Her grandma tried to keep her face neutral like she was a psychiatrist and Alete was her patient, but underneath, she could tell that Ammie was leading her somewhere. "Why not admit it?"

"Because I'm afraid. I *can't* love him. It could never work out between us, so loving him is just a good way to cause me pain."

"Are you sure it wouldn't work out?"

She nodded. "I'm sure. We argue all the time. And do you know what? I don't even feel bad about it. I enjoy the challenge of having someone push from the opposite side of my opinion. It fuels me and it helps me to figure out and put to words exactly what I really believe in."

"So then why is that a bad thing?"

She rolled her eyes. "Come on. Don't make me state the obvious." Her grandma just waited patiently, though, so eventually, she huffed and said, "Because, in really great marriages, the couple doesn't argue."

"Are you sure about that?"

"Of course I'm sure. Besides, even if we didn't argue so much, Ammie, I like my independence. I like to be able to do what I want, when I want, and I don't want anyone interfering with that."

Ammie studied her. "There's something more that you haven't told me. Something else fueling this anger."

Alete looked down. "He went off and spent the money for the festivals, and didn't even tell me."

"No. He just sat back, watching you do all the preparations you've done, and didn't say anything?"

Alete let herself fall back into slumping against the back of the couch as the thought stole away all of her energy. "Not exactly. We agreed not to talk about work— or really, about the stuff that we disagreed on— when we weren't at work. So we've just kind of not been talking about it at all. It was nice to, you know, just get to know him and not argue."

"And you were okay with this plan?"

Alete could hide thoughts in her brain just fine, and turn away if she ever got too close, but she never lied to Ammie. And Ammie always made her feel safe enough to open locked doors and see what was inside. Even if what was behind the door was scary or hard.

"If I'm being honest with myself, which I haven't been

over the two weeks, then no. I'm not okay with it. Looking back, it feels like Josh all over again. Like I was hiding the essence of who I am in order to get along with someone in a relationship."

She could tell that her grandma had wisdom to share. And probably some spunk. But she stayed maddeningly quiet. Finally, Ammie said, "I know you have a list of reasons you're telling yourself why a relationship with Zane won't work out. You've been telling yourself them for so long that you don't even know if they're true or if they're just what you've always believed. Will you do something for me?"

Alete hesitated and then nodded. This was Ammie asking, after all.

"You go home and get real quiet with yourself. Don't rehash the events of the past. I want you to just let yourself feel. Don't go over all the things you've been spouting, either—just *feel*. Nothing else. Got that? Now stop looking at me like I might be a little crazy. I've lived a lot longer than you, and I know things."

Alete let out a soft breath of a chuckle.

"Now go. Go feel."

"You'll be okay if I go?"

"The vertigo is gone, and I've got my medicine right here," she said, waving her phone. "This is also a way to get you here in sixty seconds if I have a problem. Go."

Alete nodded, headed three houses down to the house

that was once her grandma's, and walked into the comfort of the home that had sheltered her from any problem that had seemed too big for her to handle, ever since she was old enough to find her way there.

She sat down on her favorite couch in the living room and forced herself to shove aside any thoughts of conversations she'd had with Zane and just sat in silence.

At first, all of her brainpower was spent trying to keep thoughts of the past away. Then there was just a fuzzy nothingness as her brain— which didn't know how to do anything other than think at the rate of a hundred miles an hour— tried to figure out how to do this silent thing. As she managed to keep any rehashing of events away, she seemed to settle into a place of calm openness.

And that was when the feelings started tumbling in. Feelings that made a fire burn in her chest causing an intense longing, making her come alive at the challenge, lit her with excitement, and made her want to do more, be more, love more.

When she stopped actively thinking of things that happened between Zane and her, memories she hadn't been thinking of started tumbling in with those feelings. Times that weren't necessarily ones of her and Zane being on exactly the same page, but ones that brought her joy nonetheless.

Even looking at every interaction they'd had since that first one when she'd been on the ladder at All Nestled Inn, she realized that they held more joy, wonder, contentedness, excitement, and happiness than they held disagreements and frustrations.

The more those memories came in, the clearer she could see how he had been her idea of the perfect man from the start— she just hadn't allowed herself to feel them because she had labeled him as the enemy. Or because she was so convinced that a healthy relationship could never happen for her.

She loved that he had things so important to him that he wanted to pour all of his time, energy, focus, and strength into making them happen. It was a quality she'd always admired, and when she hadn't been focused on disagreeing with *how* he was trying to make things happen, she admired it in him.

And she loved that what he was passionate about also focused on helping people to have what had been missing the most from his childhood: safety and security. He could've let his experiences with his family make him bitter and pull away from people, but instead, he sought out a job where he could give others what he hadn't gotten. He hadn't chosen the highest-paying job; he chose the job where he could do the most good.

And she loved how willing he was to stand up for what he believed in. She hadn't spent much of her life trying to figure out what she wanted in a future husband. The "marriage will never work out for you" voice always spoke up so soon, and she never pushed past them to think about it. It had seemed pointless if she wasn't ever going to need that information.

But if she had, one of the things at the top of her list would be that he didn't let people steamroll over his opinions, or someone who was like grass in a field, bending whichever way the wind— or whoever was around him— blew.

She wanted someone with strong convictions. Someone who wasn't afraid of a debate. Someone who stood up for what he believed in even when it wasn't popular or easy.

And she loved how his standing up for what he believed in pushed her. Challenged her. Made her be better. And she loved him for it.

That was saying nothing about how attracted to the man that she was. How beautiful he was, how great he smelled, how much the air itself seemed to crackle with electricity whenever they were near to each other.

And their kisses! Just underneath the surface, they held the promise of something amazing. A relationship among the greats, if she could manage to get over her own shortcomings long enough for it to happen.

She stood up and threw the pillow she had been clutching tight to her chest against the couch. Then she yelled, probably loud enough for Ammie to hear her three houses up, "Ammie! Why did you tell me to do this?!"

Because now she got it. She fully understood what she was missing out on by not having Zane in her life. And having the knowledge that they could be great but not being able to act on it because of her own faults and fears filled her with more sorrow and regrets than she knew how to handle.

She liked who she was. She liked that she was bold and daring and willing to try new things. She liked that she could get an idea, imagine all the possibilities, and plow her way forward to make the idea a reality before most people would've even decided if it was an idea worth pursuing. She liked that she went all-in on things and didn't let obstacles get in her way. She liked that she was strong and confident.

But although she loved all those parts about herself, they didn't come without their downsides, too. After all, it meant that she was too tied to her independence to succeed in a partnership, had grown up with too much experience with a perfect marriage to want anything less, and was too headstrong to get along with someone enough to have her own perfect marriage.

She couldn't change who she was.

Even if that meant failing at a relationship with the man who could add untold depths of happiness, fulfillment, and challenge to her life.

twenty-one

ZANE

After Zane and his crew packed up all the equipment from the safety event into his truck, Jarred's truck, and onto the two side-by-sides that they used for search and rescue, they headed back to the fire station. He pulled into the unused second bay, leaving room for the other vehicles to pull in behind him.

When he got out of his truck, he headed straight to Ranger's kennel and opened the door. He crouched down, balancing on the balls of his feet, and rubbed the sides of the dog's neck. "You're such a good boy, Ranger. Thanks for waiting here for me so patiently." Ranger seemed to sense that he was distressed, so he nuzzled in closer, nearly knocking Zane over in his attempt to comfort him.

The other truck pulled in right behind his truck, and the side-by-sides pulled into the open space to the side of the trucks. He joined his crew and Stockton and the nine of them unloaded all of the equipment and got it stored away.

He thanked the firefighters and EMTs for being so willing to share their expertise and time in helping to set up and carry out a successful event and sent them on their way. He had almost gotten back to his office when he heard his name. He turned around to see Stockton walking toward him—he hadn't realized the old Chief hadn't left with the others.

"How ya doing?"

Zane shrugged.

"Hey, sorry about the Chandlers. You did a great thing today. You heard their praise, even if they didn't aim in the right direction. People know it was all you, and most don't have any trouble recognizing that."

"Thanks, Stockton."

He walked into his office to set down all his papers from the event, Ranger on his heels. Stockton followed them in and took his customary seat on Zane's mini fridge. "So, uh, I saw the exchange between you and Alete."

Zane's breath hitched, but he recovered quickly enough that he didn't think Stockton noticed. He arranged the papers on his desk, not looking in Stockton's direction. "Oh yeah?"

"That's rough, man. I'm sorry."

"Don't worry, Stockton. I can find a way to get the job done without her help."

"I have no doubt you will. You seem to have figured out how to work with this town just fine. I'm just sorry that, you know."

He looked at Stockton.

"Back when me and Kathleen were dating, we broke up once, too. It was painful."

Zane picked up some papers that probably needed filing and turned his back on Stockton to put them in their folders. Eventually, he finished, though, so he took a deep breath and turned to face Stockton. "I understand why she's upset. She was at the hospital with her grandma and that's about as valid of a reason for not showing up as you could get. Yet, I was a jerk about it."

Ranger walked over to sit at Zane's feet, and he reached down and scratched just under his collar.

"What's the rest of the reason?"

"I was a bigger jerk for not telling her that I spent the festival money to buy the trailer, communications equipment, emergency supplies, and triage kits. I guess I kind of hoped that the city council or Mayor Stone would've told her for me since they approved it."

He sunk into his chair. "And I guess I didn't want to because I knew that we would argue over it and I was kind of enjoying a couple of weeks of just basking in the relationship without worrying about that stuff.

It was cowardly, I know. There's so much this town needs that we could've used five times that amount. For the bare necessities, though, we needed that money. It wasn't like I wanted it to build a throne room or something trivial. This is equipment to save lives."

"So why do you think she fought it?"

"She says that town events are important for town bonding. But since I've been here, I've planned several events where the town has gotten a chance to bond. That has to at least come close to making things even. I mean, I planned them as bonding activities because that's what *she* wanted me to do."

It was exasperating. He was doing everything he could to make this town safe and prepared— the town she loved so much— but he couldn't win.

"No, you did those town activities because you found out that was the way this town would respond and do what you wanted them to do, and you wanted results. Doing them was the only way to meet *your* goals."

Stockton's words felt like someone punching him in the gut. Is that what he'd done? He paused. If he was being painfully honest, it probably was.

"And she has helped you with it all— even when you two didn't get along."

Another punch to the gut. Zane looked down at the cement floor of his office. He was not only a jerk but he also hadn't given her nearly enough credit. Not by a long shot.

"Have you thought about what she wants? I'm betting you have a good idea of why all the festivals and events are important to her or you wouldn't have gone in the direction you have with the emergency preparedness. But do you know why the Thankful for You festival is especially important to her?"

"No." He knew she was in charge of it and had assumed that was the reason why it was important. But she probably wouldn't be in charge of it year after year if there wasn't more to it than that. And he hadn't even asked. All those chances he'd had to find out more, and it hadn't occurred to him even once to be curious. "What do you know about it? Have you ever gone?"

"Yeah. I've been there for every single one since the first when Alete was just twelve."

His eyes flew to Stockton's. "Twelve?" Hadn't she told him that the first one was ten years ago? That would've put her at eighteen, not twelve.

Stockton nodded, his arms crossed over his chest, like always. "It was late November, and she had just finished cancer treatment. Did she tell you she had cancer?"

Zane nodded.

"The girl had just been through a year tougher than most of us ever have experienced. Instead of celebrating freedom after having cancer take it away, do you know what she did? She planned the very first Thankful for You event.

"She invited all her family, friends, neighbors— everyone who she considered part of her support group while going through treatment— to come to a 'thankful feast' at her house on the day before Thanksgiving. Along with the help of her parents and probably her siblings, she made a meal fit for a king.

"So we all showed up at her house, and they had tables everywhere. I mean *everywhere*. They must have borrowed some from the church. They were in the kitchen, dining room, foyer, living room, and even in the hallways. And each place was set with its own little name card of who should sit there.

"And every single person's plate— and mind you, there were a lot of us— she had covered with yellow sticky notes listing all of the specific-to-that-person reasons why she was thankful for them."

Zane tried to keep his emotions in check as Stockton's voice got deep and gravelly and filled with emotion. He realized that the story didn't surprise him at all. Alete was just the kind of person who would've done something like that at twelve.

"She didn't only do it that first year to thank us for helping her get through her fight with cancer. She invited us back every single year, and every year, our plates were covered with sticky notes, sharing all the new ways she was thankful for us.

"Then, when she was ready to go off to college, she asked her parents if she could go with them to a Main Street Business Alliance meeting, and pitched having them take over her tradition as a new town tradition.

"Of course, they said yes. No question. But no one has Alete's gift for bringing out the best in people. The tradition stayed alive, but just barely."

"And she took it over again when she came back from college?"

Stockton nodded. "But with a few changes. She said she knew how great it made her feel when she did the sticky notes for everyone and she wanted others to have that same feeling. So instead of the notes on the plates, she turned it into a week of service.

"She wrote an article for the paper asking people to seek out ways they could serve other people in the town, secretly or not, and said if they needed ideas, she had a list at Keetch's Burgers and Shakes of people who could use various help. And the list was long because she didn't want people to not serve simply because they ran out of ideas.

"She said that people who wanted to thank others for doing service for them could write it on a yellow sticky note and stick it in the window of Keetch's so everyone could see. Then she had the Thankful Feast right on Main Street in front of Keetch's."

"Forty people showed up that year," Zane said, remembering what she had told him.

Stockton nodded. "Which was probably close to the same number she had in those years when she was a kid living at home. You should see it now, though." He shook his head. "That girl of ours has the golden touch. *Nine hundred* people came last year.

"Now, mind you, this is a town event only— we don't do this to bring in tourists. And with a population the size of Nestled Hollow, you can see how impressive that is. The tables went all the way down both sides of Main Street from one end to the other. Everyone donates what they can, and she organizes teams of several dozen volunteers to cook the food and dish it up for that many people.

"And now, during the week of Thanksgiving, those yellow Thankful for You sticky notes cover every inch of space on every window of every business on Main Street. We no longer need the long lists of people to help—she got us all into the habit of looking out for ways we could help each other all on our own.

"This town wouldn't be what it is if it wasn't for her. She changed us. She changed all of us."

Zane swallowed back the emotion. "She changed me, too," he whispered. He knew it now, but he hadn't noticed it at first. Thinking back to who he was when he first stepped out of his truck the day he moved into town, and then comparing it to who he was now, it was easy to see how massive the change had been.

And all he could do to thank her was to fight her on the things that mattered the most to her. And try to rob the town of the thing that changed them the most. He had definitely been a jerk. It was amazing that it took her so long to walk away from helping him.

Zane's chest burned with a deep longing. The regret of missing out on something amazing. The sorrow of not realizing how much he enjoyed having Alete in his life before she was gone. And the heartache of having continually tried to break a relationship with her, even before it got started.

How could he have been so stupid and bull-headed and wrong? Not just today, but for months? He could feel the remorse and grief hitting him hard, and he didn't want Stockton to see exactly how much it was wrecking him.

Luckily, the man knew when to leave. He stood up and started to walk out, but paused at the edge of Zane's desk, his back to Zane. Without saying a word, he pulled a coin out of his pocket and sat it at the corner of his desk. He waited a moment, then flipped it over and walked away.

Stockton had known Zane would flip to the love side of the coin all those weeks ago. How hadn't Zane known?

Then he realized he had known, clear back on that first day in Nestled Hollow when he checked in at All Nestled Inn.

twenty-two

ALETE

Alete realized that she hadn't ever— not a single time in her life— gotten to the point in a relationship where she really *really* wanted things to work out. She was always the first one to call things off. This time, though, she wanted it with everything she had.

She texted a couple of friends who seemed to be really good at the dating and relationship thing but they just suggested that she find a way to show him that she did want to work out their differences and be in an actual relationship. But neither of them had given any advice on how she, Alete Keetch, could actually make a relationship work.

She glanced at the clock— it was just past nine. Her parents should be home from her brother's house by now, and she knew they were who she really needed to talk to.

Plus, she wanted to make sure that Ammie was still okay. So she slipped on some shoes and a jacket and walked in the moonlight and chirping crickets the short distance to her parents' house.

Her parents and Ammie were all in the kitchen, Ammie wearing her nightgown and her parents at the counter, making brownies.

"It's a little late for brownies, isn't it?"

Her mom glanced at her dad and they shared a smile. "Usually. But as we were driving home from Nate's and Hope's house, we were almost to the Nestled Hollow exit, and your dad said, 'Do you know what I'm in the mood for?' So I said, 'Brownies?' because that's what I was in the mood for, and it turns out that's exactly what he was in the mood for, too!"

Of course, it was. And of course, they were making them together. It was like a string attached the two of them, making them want to be together no matter what they were doing. They even went grocery shopping together.

"Then when we got home," her mom said, "Ammie told us you broke up with Zane. We figured you'd be over before long, so the brownies seemed like an extra good idea."

Her dad scraped the batter into the baking dish. "And from what we can gather, the two of you should be together."

"Well, *now* I know that." She plopped down on one of the bar stools and then reached a finger across the counter to get a swipe of brownie batter. She licked it off her finger but didn't even taste it.

She just needed to admit everything. Get it all out. "It's too late, though, because I already ruined everything. The things he wants to do for this town are great and important. And I was so caught up in being angry at how he was wanting to pay for whatever he thought that we needed that I didn't stop to listen or understand or really even ask about what was needed or why the town needed it. I know him well enough to know that they were probably life-saving things. But I didn't care, because I wanted my festival. I wasn't being fair."

Her dad nodded as he slid the brownies into the oven and closed the door. "Those are good things to realize. But I don't see how you could've ruined everything. All you have to do is go tell him you want to understand more and see what you can do to support him. Piece of cake. Problem solved."

"Not solved. Because, Dad, it isn't just about me realizing that I'm in love with him and probably have been for quite a while now. It's..." How could she explain? "It's that Zane is a forever kind of man."

Not that they had talked about that at all. But from how well she did know him and from hearing what his childhood was like, it wasn't hard to guess that he wasn't likely to invest in a relationship where he didn't think the other person was going to commit to fully being there always.

More than that, though, she knew enough about herself and about her experience over a dozen years of dating casually and more seriously— even being engaged— that Zane was different. When it came to him, she was a forever kind of woman.

"I would love a forever with Zane. I would love to be the kind of person who could actually have a 'forever' with someone, but I'm just...not."

Her mom came around the counter and sat on the barstool next to her. "What makes you say that?"

She snorted. "Well, for one, I'm too independent and feisty. Second, I have you two as parents. So I'm doomed to live a life alone."

Her dad came around the counter, too, and sat next to Ammie at the kitchen table. He shot a look at Ammie, but her grandma just gave him an eye roll and a head nod in Alete's direction that clearly said, "I think it's weird, too. Just listen and you'll understand."

So her dad said a simple, "Explain."

"You two are the shining example of a perfect marriage! You've shown me what it can be like. You never fight. Your thoughts are eerily in sync. You both want to spend every waking hour with one another. You've got the same interests. You look out for each other. It's like neither of you even needs to mention that you have an itch on your back before the other is already scratching it."

Her parents shared expressions of confusion. Identical expressions of confusion, of course. Like looking in the mirror. Then her dad turned to her. "Let me make sure I've got this. You don't think you can ever get married because your parents have a good marriage?"

"Yes!"

"I think you've got that backward, dear," her mom said. "You're supposed to not want to get married if your parents have a terrible marriage."

Alete rubbed her hands over her face and laughed. She knew how crazy this sounded. "I know, but listen. You've shown me how great marriage *can* be. I know the kind of person I am, and I know I can't pull this off. And if I know I can't, how could I ever get married? I would be miserable, knowing that this—" she motioned between her parents, trying to encapsulate their entire relationship, "—was possible, but also knowing it was forever out of reach."

"Oh, honey," her mom said, reaching out with both hands and grabbing hold of hers. "Our marriage hasn't always been this way. Sure, we're best friends and we share everything with each other, but it hasn't always been easy. We started out liking some of the same things, and over the course of being married a whole lot of years, our interests have kind of grown into a broader set that encompasses both our interests. Since we do so much together, that's why we tend to have a lot of the same ideas and thoughts go through our minds."

"But we didn't start out being made for each other," her dad said.

Ammie put her fist down on the table. "Well, ain't that the truth!" Then she laughed, and her parents chuckled, too.

"You really didn't?"

"Nope," her mom said, and suddenly she couldn't believe that there was this big part of her parents' lives that she didn't really know much about.

"How did you get from not being made for each other to where you are now?"

"Because we realized that marriage wasn't about having the same opinions or thinking the same thoughts. It wasn't about wanting the other person to be who we wanted them to be, and it wasn't about making sure our own needs were taken care of.

"We decided that in our relationship, we weren't going to worry about whether or not the other person was perfect, and we were always going to each put the other person's needs first. So I don't have to worry if my own back itches— I only worry about your mom's, because I know she has my back."

It struck her that in so many conversations with Zane,

she was trying to get him to understand that the people in their community weren't perfect, but they did look out for each other, and that was what mattered. All along, her parents had been showing her the same thing. She knew the concept deep in her core, and it influenced everything she did in Nestled Hollow. Somehow she missed that it also applied to her and her relationships.

"I'll let you in on a little secret," her dad said. "In the car on the way home tonight, when I said, 'Do you know what I'm in the mood for,' my answer wasn't brownies. It was actually watching an episode of *Law and Order* before bed. I didn't get in the mood for brownies until after your mom suggested it."

"Edward!"

Her dad smiled at her mom. "Don't tell me you don't do the same thing."

Her mom chuckled and held her hand up beside her mouth to block her lips from her dad's view and said in a loud whisper, "I do the same thing all the time."

"You guys do not."

"We do, too. I guess the cat's out of the bag now."

"Okay, I've been nice and quiet for an impressively long time," Ammie said. "I think I should get a medal— or at least first pick of the brownies— and a turn to tell you what's up. You think that being independent and feisty means you can't be a 'forever' person?"

Alete had been so busy having her mind blown at her

parents' marriage confessions that she hadn't been thinking at all about the other faults she had that were stopping her. "They're just things that make me not so compatible with an equal partnership or marriage."

"Says who? Would you call me independent?"

Alete let out a single breath of a laugh. "As independent as they come. I'm pretty sure I got it from you."

"How about feisty?"

"You've got that in spades, Ammie."

"Well, I'll tell you that I've never lost either of those, yet me and Frank got along famously. Ask anyone." Her parents were nodding. "But I swear we agreed on diddly squat. And we both enjoyed hobbies that the other hated.

"That didn't mean we didn't get along, though. I loved your grandpa as fiercely as the day is long, and he loved me the same, and neither of us ever had to wonder otherwise. You know this. You spent enough time at our house as a child to see all the sides of us. It's been seven years since he passed, and my love for him hasn't lessened a speck."

She knew her grandparents were happily married. It was obvious to everyone. Why hadn't she realized that for her entire childhood, she'd had an example right under her nose of someone feisty and independent whose marriage was still amazing?

Her dad got up to check on the brownies, then shut the oven door again. "Some of the most successful people

I know are successful *because* they have marriages where they challenge each other and push each other to grow. Not everyone enjoys debating. For some people, it feels like conflict to them. But those who do should be with someone who also enjoys it."

"You're not us," her mom said. "Your marriage can be just as strong without looking like ours."

For someone who sought out and craved freedom, she hadn't realized how much her beliefs about marriage had been chaining her down.

Finding out that she didn't have to have someone perfectly in sync with her to have a relationship like her parents had felt like a massive weight being lifted off her shoulders. She could still be who she was, find the man who was so perfect for her right in the lobby of her inn, and if they put each other first, they could have their forever.

She, Alete Keetch, was capable of having a forever. She got off the barstool. "So what do I do to make things right with Zane?"

Ammie shrugged. "Well, you mentioned that you haven't tried to understand the hot fire chief's side of spending the festival funds. Maybe start with that."

twenty-three

ZANE

Zane was coughing and feverish. He drifted in and out of consciousness, but he wasn't sure he'd heard his brother come home yet. He knew he should get up and check that the doors were still locked, but he was so tired and so sick and too exhausted to make his legs work.

Then it was morning, and he got out of bed, wondering why Oliver wasn't jumping on him, wishing him good morning, and begging to be taken outside. He wandered into the family room, and by the looks on his parents' faces, he knew something was wrong, and he knew that he didn't want them to say it out loud. But they did anyway.

"Honey, Oliver is gone."

The words made him fall to the ground, a heap of grief and loss and sadness. The feelings were acute and painful and instead of dulling over time, they just grew bigger and stronger and deeper and sharper.

He stood up with the body of the man he was now, no longer the thirteen-year-old boy, and realized he wasn't in his childhood home anymore. He was in his office at the fire station, and the crushing feelings weren't because of the loss of Oliver; they were because of the loss of Alete.

He woke up, threw off the covers, and sat upright, his breaths coming in gasps, his pulse racing, his body sweating. Ranger must've heard his distress and was on his bed in a second, nuzzling into him and whimpering. He stroked the dog's neck and back, over and over, trying to shake off the dream.

The part about Oliver was something he'd processed and learned to accept years ago, but the part about Alete was too new, too real, too painful, and he knew that the effects of the dream wouldn't go away anytime soon.

"What do you say, boy? Want to go for a run?" Ranger barked what seemed to be an anything-to-cheer-you-up "Yes," so Zane got out of bed and pulled on sweatpants, socks, his running shoes, a shirt, and a hoodie. And, because it was still so dark outside, a clip-on flashlight.

The morning was chilly enough that his breath came out in little puffs, just visible by the light of the moon and street lights. His apartment wasn't far from the base of the mountain, so they walked up the two blocks on paved streets until they reached the running path that led right along the line where the mountain met the town and his muscles warmed up enough to pick up the pace.

He and Ranger jogged past the burn scar and stayed on the path until they reached a trail that led up into the mountain. He'd taken the trail several times in one of the NHFD's side-by-sides in search of a wounded or lost or stranded camper or hiker. Between the light from the moon and the light from his flashlight, he could see the trail well enough that he knew he wouldn't break a leg on a protruding rock or rut in the path.

His legs burned as he jogged up the trails, especially the steeper parts as they switched back, his mind continually going from thinking about the thirteen-year-old him to the present-day him. He knew that his childhood had left him with some issues. He wasn't naive enough or unaware enough to think otherwise. But as an adult, he consciously and consistently tried to make the right decision instead the decision his childhood would've dictated that he make.

As a kid, he had coped with the loneliness and uncertainty about where he fit in by being the one who looked out for everyone else and protected them. As an adult, he was drawn to that even more strongly and took comfort in protecting those around him even more. He had taken on the mantle of being in charge of protecting his family at age nine, and since then, he had thrown himself into learning everything he could. He was used to being in charge.

He didn't want to be the kid he'd been who would do anything to get positive attention or to gain recognition. He didn't want to believe that he could only trust himself and that no one would ever be there for him. But even though he didn't want to be, he still found himself falling back on those old habits when things got hard.

But none of that excused the way he treated Alete and the things that mattered most to her. His sole focus had been on protecting people, and now towns, for so long that he hadn't even realized that he had been blind to everything else. Even when it was staring him in the face.

He pushed himself harder up the trail, making himself ignore the protesting from his legs and lungs as the surroundings slowly lightened and his path became more clear. He had been in the presence of an incredible woman since the day he first came to Nestled Hollow, and he had been so focused on his own thing that he hadn't realized it until it was too late.

No, that wasn't true. There had been so many times in her presence that he had marveled at her. So many times when he'd realized how happy and more at peace he was when he was around her. So many times he had been grateful that she had pushed him and challenged him to become better. So many times he'd admired and loved her.

He had definitely realized how incredible she was. He'd just let his own stubbornness get in the way of it all.

He and Ranger reached the end of the path near their mountain top as the sun was just starting to poke its head over the top of the mountain he stood on, its rays lighting up the tip of the mountain on the other side of I-70.

He sat down on a large flat boulder, catching his breath, and shrugged off his water pack. He pulled the little bowl out of the zippered pocket, then placed it on the ground and filled it with water. Ranger lapped the water while Zane guzzled down some from the spout of his pack.

The valley between the mountain peaks spread out below him, and he could see all of Nestled Hollow as it was starting to come awake. Ranger finished his water and made his way up the short incline next to Zane, his paws scrabbling on the loose dirt and rocks, and then onto Zane's boulder, nudging him to the edge so he could sit next to him and lay his head on Zane's lap. Zane stroked the dog's fur as he looked out at the scene below.

When he'd first come to Nestled Hollow and stood at the base of this mountaintop with Stockton, he remembered thinking how uninterested he was in having any kind of relationship. He had his path planned and hadn't wanted it complicated by anyone. He hadn't trusted people to be on his side, so he hadn't wanted to let them in. He'd just wanted to keep climbing the ladder he'd chosen— to be the emergency management director here, and then in a bigger city, and eventually a state capital.

But he also knew that Alete would likely want to always live in Nestled Hollow. Was he willing to give up his dreams of other cities?

Did he have to give it up? He tried to pull back the layers of fears he'd had since his youth, and just tried to think of Alete and what giving himself fully to a relationship with her would mean. What that would be like.

Just like the rest of his adult life, he didn't want past fears to rule future decisions. Did he trust that his dreams were safe with Alete? That if he shared them with her, together they would find a way to make all of their dreams work?

Was he willing to put his trust in someone to be there for him? He realized that, in sharing his life with someone else, his plans might change. Did he trust that he would be happy with those changes? That he might even be happier with them than he would've been otherwise?

Maybe it all came down to a single question: Did he trust Alete?

An overwhelming peace fell over him. He didn't know the answers to all his questions, and he didn't know where the future would take him. But he did know, without a doubt, that he trusted Alete, and that he trusted that his life would be a million times better if he let down those shields he had been dutifully keeping in place for so long and shared his life with her.

And he wanted her to be able to trust him just as fully. He wanted to be there for her in everything.

"Did you know I loved Alete from the start?"

Ranger gave a quiet bark in answer.

"Of course you did. Did you ever think to tell me? Because that information would've been nice to know. Maybe it would've helped me not be a jerk. Repeatedly."

Ranger whimpered.

"It's not your fault." He reached out and gave him a good rub. "It's only mine. You're a good boy, Ranger."

After a few minutes, he said, "But she is pretty great, isn't she?"

Ranger yipped. He never yipped. It sounded like he was trying to give a happy "Yep!"

"So what do I do? How does someone go about repairing the damage they've done practically every moment since the one where they met someone? Because I'm pretty sure this isn't a bouquet of flowers and box of chocolate kind of thing. It's going to take something a lot bigger than that."

And then suddenly he knew. The town needed the equipment he bought— there was no question about that. But for as much as he'd thought the festivals were trivial at the beginning, he understood now how much they all needed it. It wasn't that Alete wanted them for herself;

she simply knew how much the town needed them, and she dedicated her life to helping them get what they needed. He got that now.

He felt pretty confident that he had exhausted all other ways to get the money for the equipment. But there had to be a way for him to find the money for the festivals. If not for all of them, at least for the Thankful for You one. He had no idea how, but he would find a way.

Then, even if she never wanted to see him again, at least he would know he hadn't taken the Thankful for You festival from her or from the town.

As he and Ranger headed back down the mountain, he couldn't get down fast enough. Yesterday, he'd felt that there was no chance of recovering what he'd let foolishly slip through his fingers.

Today, as he watched the sun spilling its light further down the mountain with each passing moment, he felt hope. Hope that maybe if he tried enough, he could convince Alete to want to give a relationship with him another chance. And he was going to do everything he could to help that happen.

twenty-four

ALETE

In the early morning hours, just after waking up, the thought had popped into Alete's mind that she'd had plenty of time to text Zane while she'd been in the hospital with Ammie, but she had pushed it aside each time. It wasn't like her at all to not let someone know if she couldn't show up to something, so she'd lain in bed, letting herself explore why.

In a realization that had shocked and surprised and pained her, she'd discovered that she hadn't texted because she'd been letting fear grab the steering wheel. She'd known what the event meant to Zane, and because she had been afraid to continue the relationship, she'd subconsciously sabotaged it.

Now that she understood those fears, though, she was

done letting them drive. Now she just wanted to understand more fully this man that she had fallen for.

But as much as she wanted to know about the equipment and supplies that Zane purchased with the festival money, she felt like she needed to do something more than simply ask him to tell her. She needed to *show* that she understood it was important to him, instead of only worrying about what was important to her.

So she met with Mayor Stone and found out that Zane's communications trailer was more than just a really large, expensive cell phone or walkie-talkie. It would allow them to communicate with county and state agencies, even when all normal routes of communication had been cut off.

It also contained first aid equipment and supplies and triage kits that could be easily taken on-site in places where the ambulance couldn't go. But some of the money was for things like an emergency alert system, training for citizens, and events to prepare everyone.

The more she and the mayor talked, the more she realized how much Zane had worked to prepare Nestled Hollow specifically, and how he had looked out for them in every capacity. His proposal was pared down to the most essential and took everything into consideration.

It was a thing of beauty, really. The mayor and city council had recognized that, too, which was why they had given him the town budget to look at. Especially after the fire and knowing what spring might bring, they all knew that the time to act was now. They told him that if he could find the money somewhere, they would support him unquestionably.

It all made her feel guilty that she hadn't tried harder to understand. Instead of stopping Zane, she should've been supporting him all along. She should've handed him the Thankful for You event on a silver platter to show that she was willing to give up the thing that was nearest and dearest to her heart because she believed in him and what he was doing.

It wasn't exactly hers to give, of course. It had become the town's long ago. But she should've removed all the obstacles that she'd been placing in his path since that first day in the combined City Council and Main Street Business Alliance meeting.

It pained her to see the event go, and it did still worry her that the event would lose its momentum. But after learning all she had, instead of being mad that it was taken from her, she wished she could go back in time and give it up in order to apologize to the man she loved for not being willing to look at his side of things. And to hopefully convince him to give the two of them a second chance at being a couple.

Now all she could do was apologize, offer her support, and hope he was willing to give them another shot. She picked up her phone to text him. Her fingers hovered over the screen, shaking slightly as the right words didn't come to mind. She hadn't seen or talked to him in two days, and she wasn't sure how he'd react. Maybe the right words never would come, so she just typed.

> Alete: I'd love to talk. Can you meet me on the pedestrian bridge closest to All Nestled Inn?

His reply was quick, which was good because her heart was breakdancing and she didn't know how long it could keep it up.

> Zane: I'm out on a call right now. Can we meet there at 5:30 instead?

She glanced at the clock at the top of her cell phone— it was just after four. She responded with a simple *Yes*, set her phone down, and breathed deeply. Then she got up to go find some work to do in the inn because if she sat there waiting, her heart couldn't take it.

———

At five twenty-five, Alete put on her jacket and walked out to the pedestrian bridge that led over Snowdrift Springs, linking one side of Main Street to the other. She could've asked Zane to meet her anywhere, or she could've even shown up in his office at the fire station, but somehow it felt fitting to bridge their differences on a literal bridge. There was the whole water under the bridge metaphor, too, but simply standing on the bridge was probably already overkill on the metaphors.

Her heart was pounding and she really hoped her antiperspirant was doing its job.

A couple of minutes before five thirty, she spotted him as he came around the side of the clock tower that straddled Snowdrift Springs, partially hiding the fire station from view, and headed her direction.

He was dressed in his fire chief uniform and the sight of him stole her breath. His stride was confident and strong and she swore the clouds parted from the evening sun just to cast light on him.

As he neared, she could see that he was wearing the partial smile that she loved so much, but there was something else there, too. Nerves, maybe? Or maybe not. That stride had shown nothing but unwavering sureness.

"Hi, Zane," she said as he stepped onto the bridge.

"Hi, Alete," he said, and he looked at her like he was taking her in for the first time, and her heart kicked up a notch.

"Zane, I haven't been fair, and I want to apologize."

He raised an eyebrow.

"You have amazing things planned for this town. Carefully thought out, essential, incredible plans, and I never even stopped being upset about losing the festivals to truly find out about them. After talking with Mayor Stone to find out everything, it's obvious why they hired you. They knew Nestled Hollow deserved what only you could give."

She paused long enough to see the pleased, hopeful look on his face, and then, in a bold move, added, "And I love you for it."

The look on his face turned immediately to surprise which looked rather adorable on him. He cocked his head to the side. "Did I hear that right? Did you just say you love the enemy?"

She laughed and gave him a playful shove to the shoulder. "I was every bit as surprised as you are. But looking back, I guess I shouldn't have been. I mean, you are pretty perfect."

That half-smile turned into a full grin. "Except for all the parts where I disagreed with you."

"Actually, I realized that's a big part of what makes you perfect. I like that you'll stand up for what you believe and that you'll fight for the things you know are worth fighting for. And I like that when you challenge me, it pushes me to be better."

"Even when it means me taking away your festival?"

"It's not my festival. I gave it to the town ten years ago. But let's pretend we could go back in time." She held out her palms, cupped and pressed together like she held something. "This is me, giving away all my objections to the festival money being used for emergency preparedness. I would've wrapped it all pretty with a bow before giving it to you, but I couldn't find a box that was the right size."

He chuckled and acted like he was taking the present from her hands as if it was a treasure. Then he looked up and she saw how much it affected him clearly on his face. "Thank you for this. I know how much the Thankful for You festival means to you, and I'm touched and honored that you'd give it up. Nobody has ever..." He swallowed hard. "Thank you."

"I get it now, Zane. I understand what you've been trying to do for this town, and I'm sorry I was doing so much to try to stop you. Not that I had any actual power to stop you, of course."

He looked up and met her eyes. "I think you *vastly* underestimate the power you have."

"Maybe if I would've realized that I shouldn't be stopping you from the start, I would've noticed how much I was falling for you sooner."

He gave her a look like he was soaking in her words, and it made her heart do a little hopeful flutter that maybe he felt the same. "But think of how much fun we would've missed out on if you did that."

She smiled. "True."

He was silent for a moment, and then he pulled out his phone and texted someone, and Alete's mind raced. She had also told him that she loved him, and she was suddenly worried that he didn't want anything more from her than a professional relationship.

He slipped the phone back into his pocket. "I got you a gift, too."

"You did?"

He nodded. "I, also, would've wrapped it all pretty if I could've found the right box." He reached out and took both of her hands in his, and she thrilled at the touch that felt so right. "I want to give you back the Thankful for You festival."

"No, Zane. You spent the money the right way. The town needed it."

"And I found out just how much this town wouldn't be what it is if it weren't for you and your festival. I get how important it is now. Nestled Hollow got it a long time ago. And I want you to have it. I want the town to have it."

He looked up like he was thinking or picturing something. "You know, when I first got here, I would've had no idea what the first step would be in trying to secure funding for something like that. But then I just asked myself, 'What would Alete do?'" He smiled that playful smile, and it melted her.

"So I went to the town. I talked to dozens and dozens of residents. I went to people in town that I learned were very well off, even if they liked to keep that information quiet, and got them to donate anonymously.

"I went to the Business Alliance and asked your fellow business owners if any had extra they could give. I even asked people in town who worked outside of Nestled Hollow if they would ask the businesses they worked at for a donation.

"I asked everyone I could find. You've made a difference to this town, and they showed it by opening their wallets. Enough that the Thankful for You festival is back on."

"You're really giving me my festival? You did that for me?" She knew her smile spread clean across her face. She had accepted that she wouldn't have the event that she'd loved. But to know that he had found a way to give it to her made warmth spread through her whole body.

He smiled. A whole smile that seemed to come from soaking her in, and it looked beautiful. "You might not have known I was doing it, but I couldn't have done it without you."

"We should work together more often because, apparently, we are pretty incredible."

"That, and maybe much more." He smiled that adorable smile as he stepped closer. "I think I had an inkling of how far I was going to fall for you the first time I saw you standing one step past safe on that ladder in the lobby of All Nestled Inn. It took me a while to get it, too. But I get it now."

He brushed two knuckles along her temple and across

her jaw, and she closed her eyes to savor the touch. "I've realized that I love you so much and in so many ways that I had to write down the reasons why."

Her eyes flew open. "I'm intrigued, Chief Collins." She glanced at his pocket. "Do you have this list with you?"

He smiled and said, "It's nearby."

There had been movement on Main Street the entire time they'd been talking, but something out of the ordinary caught her eye, and she turned to see two lines of people and a lot of yellow coming from the fire station end of Main Street, one line on each side of Main Street and headed their direction.

Each person looked like they were holding something. They kept walking, spreading themselves the entire distance of Main Street. As some of them neared her— all people she knew and loved— she could see that they were all holding giant sticky notes, and all had things written on them.

She turned back to Zane. "Is this your list?"

He nodded, so she grabbed his hand and ran out to the first person holding a big yellow sticky note. She held Zane's hand as she went from person to person reading each one, smiling at the person holding the note. Each person was beaming as they watched her read them, Zane at her side.

They all started with the phrase "I'm thankful for you because," then said things like *you're thoughtful.*

You're an incredible leader.
You've got great ideas.
You're passionate about this town.
You love everyone (and I'm sure this includes Ranger ;)).
You keep me on my toes.
You bring people together.
You're passionate about tacos.
You push me to be better.
You're beautiful.
You make everything more fun.
You're compassionate.
You can debate with the best of them. (Like me. ;))
You can crush the competition in an obstacle course (including me :)).
You give everyone your heart.

On and on, sign after sign, she read more and more things he loved about her until her heart was ready to burst. Some made her laugh, some made her cry, and some made her smile up at him in awe. Then she came to the final three people— her dad, her mom, and then Ammie— and she read the signs they held.

I'm thankful for you because you want the best for people.
I'm thankful for you because you bring out the best in people.
I'm thankful for you because you bring out the best in me.

"I came to save this town," he said, "but instead, you saved me."

She looked up at this man who so fully gave himself to the things that mattered most to him and smiled. He reached out and brushed a tear from her eye ever so gently. She stepped even closer to him so that only inches separated their faces and whispered, "Thank you. Thank you for all of this, and thank you for being you."

Then, right in front of everyone, he put his hands on the sides of her face, his fingers tangling in her hair, and brought his lips to hers. His kiss was soft and warm, sweet and careful like she was something precious.

She ran her hands along those strong, protective shoulders that she loved, and along the back of his neck as his hands dropped to her back; he was pulling her close as much as she was pulling him close. She poured everything she loved about him into the kiss, urgently, needing him to know and understand just how much she loved him. He responded in a way that told her that he understood and felt the same.

Just below the surface, their first real kiss had held the promise of a future relationship among the greats. This kiss delivered on that promise.

"Whooo weee!" she heard Ammie yelling. "She's kissing the hot fire chief!"

She smiled into the kiss, and Zane chuckled. "And I," he said, "am kissing the beautiful town goddess."

"I see I've moved up in rank from town cheerleader."

"And up past town student body president. Not even 'queen' felt like enough."

He kissed her forehead, then she looked up at the face of the man she loved, the face of the man she finally realized was perfect for her. She wanted forever and she was finally ready to give it to him.

epilogue

ZANE

Alete stood by Zane's side in the open bay of the fire station, all of his crew around him. And all of them, including Zane, were sporting shaved heads. Their hair had grown back since last year, but when Principal Ploeger suggested that they make the fire drills— along with his now traditional going to school in pajamas and getting his head shaved— a yearly thing, Zane got on board along with his crew and had his head shaved at a Nestled Hollow Elementary school assembly.

"You," Alete said, running her hands over his freshly-shaved head, "make a very sexy bald man."

He grinned at her. "Anything for a good cause."

"You know, I believe it was almost a year ago when I predicted that the town emergency preparedness activities weren't just going to be a one-time thing."

Zane wrapped his arm around her waist. "Are you fishing for a 'You were right?' Because I do actually have the communications system right here. I can shout it out to the whole town."

She laughed. That loud, unrestrained, hearty laugh that he never tired of.

He breathed into her ear, "I just heard that you hated that September didn't have any town festivals, so I wanted you to have a yearly one."

She stepped on her tiptoes to plant a kiss on his lips, and he grabbed her around the waist and made it one with more meaning than a quick peck, to the roar of delight from his crew. "I just like that we get to do this one together."

"Me, too," Liam said. "It's more fun when you do."

"I'm all set to go," Jim said.

Zane looked around at his crew. "Is everyone else ready?"

All seven gave him the thumbs up, bouncing on their toes like they couldn't wait to take off and do their part in a drill of this magnitude.

The whole town knew they were doing a natural disaster drill today but no one knew the exact time. They instructed them all to go to work or school or whatever they would normally do on a Friday. When the alert came on their phones, one neighborhood would be on full evacuation and everyone else would be on evacuation notice.

For those whose neighborhood was evacuated, they could grab their Go Bags and bedding and get out quickly if they were in the neighborhood already, but if they weren't, they couldn't go back to their homes. Everyone in the other neighborhoods could go to their homes if they weren't already there to get their Go Bags and bedding.

The message they sent out would tell which neighborhoods were supposed to meet at the high school gym, which at the middle school gym, which at the elementary school, and which at the church. Since the evacuated neighborhood wouldn't have their supplies if they hadn't already been home, they would all get a chance to see how quickly they could get those people the things that they needed.

Jim was going to be radioing instructions to all the people he had trained over the past year. Judah and Liam were working with the block coordinators to make sure everyone was accounted for. Families were testing their meeting plans. Amy and Legacy were setting up mock triage centers. Tila and Jarred would take one side-by-side and Zane, Alete, and Ranger would head out in the other side-by-side, lending help where needed, and seeing how the evacuation was going.

"Send out the message!" Zane shouted, and everyone

rushed to their posts as Jim alerted the town of the beginning of the drill.

Alete, Zane, and Ranger all hopped in their side-by-side and pulled out onto Main Street, seeing the town come alive with people hurrying to do their part in the town drill. It was exhilarating to see everything that he had been working to accomplish all come together like this.

"You know," he said as he turned up toward the evacuation zone, "thirteen months ago when I first moved to Nestled Hollow, the possibility never crossed my mind that tonight I would get to take part in what I'm sure will go down in Nestled Hollow history as the largest potluck dinner we've ever experienced, followed by the largest town sleepover ever."

"Thirteen months ago when you first moved to Nestled Hollow," Alete said as she reached out and placed her hand on the back of his neck and ran her fingers along his neck, causing happy shivers to run down his spine, "the possibility that we would be getting married next month never crossed my mind, either."

"Obviously we are both luckier than we ever thought we could be thirteen months ago."

"Obviously."

He pulled off to the side of a road in an area where he thought they would need the most help evacuating and they got out of the vehicle. As they walked toward the houses, Alete wrapped her hand in his, and Ranger followed at their feet.

He thought back to the man he was thirteen months ago and knew he never would've guessed that he would be this happy, this contented, this fulfilled, and this excited about his future. He had let his shields fall when he started dating Alete, and he had given his heart fully to her. For the first time in his life, he felt like his heart was safe and protected in someone else's hands.

He smiled at the amazing woman at his side. He would very gladly be her "forever."

———

Author's note:

I hope you enjoyed seeing Alete and Zane get their happily ever after! These characters—and everyone in Nestled Hollow—were such a joy to spend time with.

I'm excited for you to read the first book in a new series! *It Started with a Sunset* is a sweet small-town romance that I think you will really love.

I wish you many hours of happy reading in your future!

—Meg

IT STARTED WITH A SUNSET

For these two workplace opposites, attraction caught them by surprise.

Summer Graham's life is just how she likes it—surrounded by people in both her personal life and in her work life as an admissions recruiter at a university. Want to go on an adventure? She's your gal. Want a serious relationship? She can probably introduce you to someone who does, but it's not her.

Brock McMillan spends his time striving for perfection,

being a good older brother, and enjoying his job helping students get college scholarships. Oh, and disagreeing with Summer on pretty much everything that goes on in the office.

Not that it's purposeful. Their ideas are just kind of like their office spaces—Brock's is minimalist and logical (but Summer will tell you it's where ideas go to die) and Summer's is lively, fun, and creative (but Brock will tell you it's chaotic).

They're teamed up to run Aquamoose Tracks together— the big overnight event put on by the Welcome Center at the university where they both work. Both think they know how it will all turn out, but they're both in for a few surprises.

And they definitely never expect to fall in love.

It Started with a Sunset is the first in a new series where a job becomes a community, coworkers become family, and the romances are sweet, swoony, and chock-full of chemistry. Each interconnected stand-alone novel has its own happily ever after.

get the series

Coming Home to the Top of Main Street

Second Chance on the Corner of Main Street

Christmas at the End of Main Street

More than Friends in the Middle of Main Street

Love Again at the Heart of Main Street

More than Enemies on the Bridge of Main Street

Listen to the audiobooks on YouTube

Meg Easton is the *USA Today* bestselling author of contemporary romances and romantic comedies with fun, memorable, swoon-worthy characters, and settings you'll want to pack up and move to. She lives at the foot of a mountain with her name on it (or at least one letter of her name) in Utah. She loves gardening, bike riding, baking, swimming before the sun rises, and spending time with her husband and three kids.

She can be found online at www.megeaston.com

Sign up to receive her newsletter and stay up to date with new releases, get exclusive bonus content, and more.

If you liked this book please leave a review. Your review can help other readers find books they might fall in love with.

youtube.com/@megeastonauthor
bookbub.com/authors/meg-easton
instagram.com/megeaston_author
facebook.com/MegEastonBooks
tiktok.com/@megeaston_author